Going Toe to Toe

Also by Yahrah St. John

Frenemy Fix-Up

Visit the Author Profile page at Harlequin.com for more titles.

Going Toe to Toe

YAHRAH
ST. JOHN

ISBN-13: 978-1-335-57480-0

Going Toe to Toe

Copyright © 2024 by Yahrah Yisrael

Harlequin Enterprises ULC
22 Adelaide St. West, 41st Floor
Toronto, Ontario M5H 4E3, Canada
www.Harlequin.com

Printed in U.S.A.

To Jackie Brown for all her help with research for this book.

One

Lyric

I'm on my way to Aruba, sitting in a first-class cabin, drinking a glass of my favorite champagne, when I see *him*. And suddenly I'm not thinking about how this getaway is what I need before my dance studio opens in a few weeks. Or how I'll be swamped by little girls in tutus and leotards, making relaxation a thing of the past. Instead, I focus on my fellow passenger, looking hot in a fitted pullover, a talisman necklace and dark jeans.

He is tall; not quite six feet, but close enough. Sexy and dangerous with smoldering eyes the color of warm honey and a short, tapered fade with a manicured beard that could easily cause a rash between a woman's thighs.

Sweet heavens!

As if somehow sensing my thoughts, his eyes connect with mine. I blush and sink into my reclining seat. He merely smiles, passes by and walks farther into the Economy cabin.

I suck in a breath. *He's* coming to Aruba? Lord, help me.

My best friends, the Gems, wanted me to have some fun before my business launches—that's why they paid for this trip—and if he's coming, there might be hope for fun yet.

And that hope for fun is still with me, even after a nearly seven-hour flight with a layover in Miami, when the front desk clerk at the Five Stars Resort and Spa on Eagle Beach tells me, with an apologetic smile, "I'm afraid there's been a mistake."

I frown, not understanding the words coming out of the clerk's mouth.

"What do you mean? I have my booking confirmation here." I hold out my phone. "It says I have a villa for the week."

The clerk takes my phone, scans it. "Yes, it does, but it appears when someone made the booking here at the hotel, they inadvertently added two people to the same reservation."

I don't see the problem. "Surely you can change it?"

I'm not prone to anger. I worked hard for years to fulfill my dreams as a dancer, and then altered those dreams and worked hard in a different way when circumstances changed. I've found it's best to be patient and calm when fighting for what you want.

"Ordinarily, we would make the change," the clerk replied, "but we're overbooked. There's no other villa available."

"Overbooked?" I ask as I hear a male voice beside me ask the same question.

It's the hottie I was drooling over on the plane ride to Aruba. When I'd grabbed my luggage off the carousel and headed to the man holding up a sign for the resort, Mr. Tall, Hot and Sexy had been close on my heels. When I spun around to face him, he'd smiled and said, "Looks like we're going to the same place."

Indeed we were. And here we are. And the resort has fucked up *royally*.

"Who is the other guest?" I ask. Perhaps I can reason with them.

The front desk clerk glances to my side. She's looking directly at the man from the plane.

No, no, no.

This can't be happening. I *need* this trip, this time away. With the dance studio opening soon, I have to clear my mind, prepare for my new path, for the future I didn't expect. And there are decisions to make about my family, too....

But I stay calm, push those concerns away for the moment and walk over to Mr. Gorgeous. "It appears we have a problem."

He looks me up and down, takes in my painted pink toenails peeking out from my sandals, all the way past my thighs to my shorts—which I had the good sense to put on after we disembarked and I learned it was eighty-plus degrees—to my smocked crop top tied between my bosoms.

"Do we?"

I'm flattered—and a little flustered—by his obvious male

appreciation, but trudge on. "Would you be willing to give up the villa? My friends went to a lot of trouble to book this vacation for me."

He snorts. "Ordinarily, I might, but I paid for this villa months ago because I wanted the peace and tranquility it provides."

We stare at each other, neither willing to give an inch.

A man wearing a linen suit and tie approaches us with a somber expression. "My name is Ross Murphy, general manager of the resort. My apologies to you both for the mishap. Here at the Five Stars Resort and Spa, we pride ourselves on excellence, and mistakes like this are few and far between. If one of you is willing to downgrade, we will comp your entire stay due to this unfortunate circumstance."

"That sounds like an excellent idea." I glance over at the hottie, expecting him to do the gentlemanly thing and accept the offer, but he doesn't.

He folds his arms across his broad chest, revealing indecently large biceps, and I find myself swallowing hard.

"I'm sorry, but it's a no-go for me," he says. "I want the villa."

Ross turns to me. "Would you be willing to downgrade to an ocean-view room?"

It sounds like a good deal, at first but then I think about the pictures of the beachfront villa the Gems showed me when they convinced me to take this trip. Steps away from pristine Eagle Beach, I'd imagined walking out onto the sand with my morning cup of coffee and finally figuring out how I wanted to handle the choices in my life.

How can I give that up?

"I'm sorry, but I want the villa, too."

Ross stares exasperatedly at both of us, unsure of what to do next.

"How many bedrooms does the villa have?" the hottie asks.

"Two," Ross states.

"How about we both stay in the villa?" the hottie suggests. "I can stay out of your way because I'm here for some self-reflection, if you can do the same?"

I don't like the idea, but if I want the villa—if I want that slow, quiet beach time to figure out my next steps—I don't have much choice. Since neither of us is willing to compromise, a feasible solution is to share the space. I'm not used to sharing a suite except with the Gems, let alone with someone of the opposite sex or someone as gorgeous as Mr. Hottie.

But part of me finds the idea appealing.

Ross frowns. "This is highly unusual, Mr...."

"Masters," the hottie announces, "Devon Masters. But it's doable, is it not?" Devon raises an eyebrow. "If she's amenable, then so am I."

"She is," I reply, looking between both men. "And by the way, if we're going to be sharing a villa, my name is Lyric Taylor."

A warm smile spreads across Devon's lips as he watches me from beneath hooded lashes. "Pleasure to meet you, Lyric."

I like how my name sounds on his tongue and try to repress the light shiver that moves through me. He's Fine with a capital *F*. Something about this man makes me want to run my fingers all over him.

Maybe a vacation hookup wouldn't be a bad thing. It would not only be pleasurable, but it'd boost my confidence with the opposite sex, given my lack of experience. I've spent years dancing and training to dance, which left little time for beach trips or vacation flings. Imagine how confident I'd be after having Devon in my bed? The thought warms my cheeks.

"Then the matter is settled." Devon turns to the manager. "If you could procure our two keys, see that our baggage is handled and of course, we will both expect a partial credit for our stay along with any complimentary amenities you could offer due to this unfortunate situation."

"Of course," Ross replies and walks over to the front desk to produce two key cards. When he's done, he hands us each one. He motions to a bellboy standing nearby. "Miguel, can you show Mr. Masters and Ms. Taylor to the villa and take care of their luggage?"

"Absolutely," Miguel responds, and turns to us. "Follow me."

"After you." Devon motions for me to precede him. I stare at him for several beats, and he does the same to me. Is it my imagination or is there a flash of heat in his eyes?

We're going to be sharing a villa for an entire week.

Maybe I don't want to stay out of his way.

As I step off the golf cart, my eyes go wide with admiration. The villa is everything I imagined it to be. Waves gently lap at the powdery sand, and it feels like I've stepped onto my own slice of paradise, albeit one I have to share.

I glance over at Devon, who has followed me to the beach and appears to be equally as mesmerized as I am. "It's beautiful, isn't it?"

He nods in agreement. "Pictures don't do it justice."

"Would you like me to give you a tour?" Miguel asks from behind us.

"Yes." We reply in unison and I can't resist laughing.

I would've thought the change in my plans and sharing the villa would bring me down. But no. Somehow the man I panted after on the plane ride is my housemate and I find myself excited about that fact.

Following Miguel inside, I'm completely blown away by the modern decor. Cherrywood double doors open into a spacious living area with wood floors, whitewashed walls and bright furniture. A hanging chair faces French doors leading to the terrace outside with a large infinity pool. The Gems outdid themselves when they picked this place.

"There's an eat-in kitchen," Miguel is saying when I return my attention to the conversation at hand. "And the fridge has been fully stocked with anything you might need during your stay."

It has all the modern amenities—a gas stove, double-sided refrigerator and microwave—but it's the stylish subway tile backsplash, oven hood, open shelving and quartz countertops that appeal to me. I run my hands across the shiny top of one counter. This place is nothing like my town house in Memphis, which could use a bit of updating.

The tour continues with Miguel showing us two nicely

appointed bedrooms with seaside-themed decor, from the hanging lights made of rope to beds made of reclaimed wood. They have a true beachy vibe. The bathrooms are oases with walk-in rainfall showers and double vanities. There is even a laundry room if we need to freshen up our clothes.

"Thank you," I say when Miguel is finished showing us the villa.

"My pleasure. If you need anything, please let me know."

This time, it's Devon who speaks and extends his hand. "Thank you, Miguel."

The door closes behind Miguel, and then it's just the two of us alone in the villa.

"What do you say we open up the champagne?" Devon inclines his head to the large basket sitting on the coffee table. "I think we deserve it, don't you?"

"Definitely." I offer a nervous laugh.

Devon Masters is *the* most attractive guy I've been around in a long time and I find myself tongue-tied. Somehow I'm not worried about sharing this villa with someone I've just met. Something about Devon makes me feel safe…

Maybe it's because I'm open to the possibility of more happening between us than sharing a space.

There are a lot of things changing in my life right now. And on this trip, I'd like to be a brand-new me who's not afraid to take risks. Who feels fully comfortable in my own skin.

As a ballerina, I endured endless taunts and jeers about my body being too muscular or curvy. The snickers behind my back that my hair was too kinky. At one point, I even followed the examples of my peers and starved myself to fit the image of how the world expected a ballerina to look.

Lucky for me, my parents caught on and put me in therapy. It's one of the many reasons I admire them. They've always told me I'm a beautiful Black princess and I should never be ashamed of that, but they also didn't hesitate to seek help when their kind words weren't enough to bolster my self-esteem.

Therapy helped me see I could love the body I was in. Some days it's easier than others.

With my insecurities, my training, rehearsals and ballet performances, relationships have been few and far between. My inexperience can sometimes make me feel awkward around the opposite sex because I don't know what to say.

That's exactly how I feel now.

I watch as Devon tears the wrapping paper off the gift basket. A note falls to the floor and I reach for it.

Live it up, Lyric.
You deserve it.
The Gems

Of course this delicious assortment of champagne and charcuterie is from them. My friends are always thinking about me, and the reminder feels good.

"Who's it from?" Devon asked. "A boyfriend? Should I be worried someone is going to come after me for sharing this villa with you?"

His question catches me off guard. Other than some heated looks, he's played it very close to the vest about whether or not he is interested in me. But surely his question means he's fishing to find out if I'm unattached?

I shake my head. "No boyfriend. And should I fear a jealous girlfriend will be knocking on the door?"

"Hardly." Devon's mouth quirks in humorless smile. "I'm divorced and my ex passed away."

He drops this info like a bomb. Unlike me, he knows what it's like to love someone, to lose someone.

"I'm sorry for your loss," I reply, not sure of what else to say. A sharp tug of pity hits me square in my chest. The emotional upheaval he's endured must have changed the entire trajectory of his life.

I've never lost someone so close to me, but I've had my hopes and dreams upended. I can sympathize with his pain.

"Thank you." He opens the bottle with a loud pop, and I rush to the kitchen to find champagne flutes. Two are sitting on one of the open shelves. I grab them and return to the living room. When Devon grasps one of the flutes, our hands touch. Something…electric surges through me.

I glance up at him and his eyes have darkened.

He felt it, too.

We don't move away, but we don't act on the feeling, either.

He pours the glasses quickly and lifts one. "Salud."

"Salud."

The bubbles of the champagne hit my taste buds, but the feeling is nothing in comparison to the way Devon is looking at me over the rim of his flute. My eyelashes flutter under the force of his direct gaze. He's not avoiding me now; he's staring right at me with undisguised interest. I feel color rising on my cheeks—because with skin the color of café au lait, my complexion shows everything.

"Wh-which room would you like?" I inquire, trying to break the spell the man has me under.

"Take whichever one you want." Devon shrugs. "I just wanted the beach." He motions to the view laid out in front of us and starts walking toward the double doors.

I want to follow him outside, but I'm afraid. Afraid of the heat of his hooded stare. Afraid of this unexpected attraction.

I'm not used to such frank male attention. The few intimate experiences I've had made me feel insecure. As a professional dancer, my work was my focus. And when I decided to be intimate, those couple of men said the same thing, that I'm some sort of ice maiden. I'm not! Nervous maybe. Inexperienced, definitely. But I would like to explore my sensual side and see what all the fuss is about.

Today, my visceral response to Devon proved I'm not impervious to attraction. I'm made of flesh and blood same as any other woman. Maybe fate brought us together. First the plane, and then the mix-up with the villa.

We were meant to be here, right now.

What would happen if I were to allow nature to take its course?

This trip is a fresh start for me. A chance to embrace a new and uncertain future as not just a former dancer but also the owner of a studio and an instructor. Not just a beloved adopted daughter, but the woman who might be ready to meet her biological mother after years of keeping that door closed.

I'm here to remember who I am and rediscover the love I had for dance—before my dreams turned to ash.

If I give in to my desire for Devon while I'm on this trip, will I be ready for what comes next?

Two

Devon

I came outside because I need some air.

I had to get away from the charged energy that being in the villa with Lyric is having on my body. Sucking in a deep breath, I finish off the rest of the champagne in my flute and wish I had some more. This attraction to my housemate for the next week is surprising but not unwanted.

I came to Aruba to get away from my life in Memphis. Lyric is as far removed from my life and responsibilities as I can get.

My sister, Chantel Dixon, urged me to take this solo vacation. She told me I need to get away from the difficulties of the last three years—the disaster of my marriage, my ex-wife's untimely death in a car accident, learning to be a single parent to my daughter. Chantel says I should "hop back in the saddle."

It's not that simple.

The failure of my marriage broke something in me. And the only way I could heal was to build impenetrable walls around my heart to protect myself from getting hurt again. Chantel knows this. But still, she hasn't let up. Kianna needs a mother, Chantel is always saying, but I don't think so. We've done just fine by ourselves. I've even learned how to do Kianna's hair. I make a mean ponytail.

This trip is supposed to help me let go of past hurts and move forward, maybe even have another committed relationship someday.

For three years, I haven't been ready to jump back into the dating world.

But today has me rethinking that.

Lyric Taylor is naturally beautiful. Her almond-shaped eyes are chestnut brown and clear, her lashes long and thick, accentuating her delicate femininity. She has elegant bone structure and full sensual lips that look as though they are ready for a kiss—*my kiss*. The rest of her is graceful and willowy with a hint of curves in all the right places.

She appeals to me. And the fire she lit inside me from the first moment I saw her on the plane is why I made the impromptu offer to share the villa. Completely out of character for me.

As was my inability to hide my attraction when we touched. I know she saw that spark. Felt it. The sexual tension in the room was palpable.

She seems reserved, even shy. I see the way she glances at me from underneath her eyelashes and the pulse beating at her neck when I'm close. Because of those responses, she doesn't strike me as the type of woman to have casual affairs, but I'm hoping she might consider one with me.

I came here to focus on me and what I want for a change. And what I want is Lyric Taylor.

When I return indoors, Lyric has made herself scarce. It's probably for the best. I'm not sure what I might have done next if she was still waiting there with those fuck-me eyes. I might have had to sample a taste...

Hunger has gripped me since I saw her. Even the lingering scent of her soft, feminine smell, like rose-scented soap, is making me hot and bothered. I'm always in complete control of my emotions, my reactions. Yet tonight, I'm restless, hot and hungry. It's all because of her.

I need to cool off.

Quickly, I grab my suitcase and roll it into the other bedroom, which is farther down the hall and on the same side as Lyric's. I wonder what she's doing on the other side of the wall, but I don't act on my curiosity. Instead, I start unpacking my clothes. Once I find my swim trunks, I undress and slide them on.

Oh yes, a refreshing dip in the sea is exactly what I need. I grab a towel from the en suite bathroom along with my swim shoes and head back to the terrace. However, I'm stopped dead as I open the French doors.

Lyric stands on the terrace wearing the ittiest bittiest bikini I've ever seen in my life. It's practically indecent. I could easily loosen the ties along the sides of her waist and clutch her round yet petite derriere, bring her closer to my straining dick. Her hair is down, revealing a mane of luxurious brown waves streaked with auburn and honey high-lights. The affect is that of a sunset. I want to run my hands through it when I bring her mouth to mine.

I cough, and Lyric turns to face me. Sweet Jesus, the front of her is even better than the back. She's wearing a triangle halter top that pushes her breasts into the shape of delicious melons I want to bite into.

"Devon!" She says my name with a start.

I swallow the giant lump in my throat. "I—I didn't mean to scare you." *I was just admiring your amazing body and thinking of all things I would like to do to you.*

"Doesn't it look amazing?" She sweeps her hair into a messy topknot, making her look even more adorable. "I was about to go for a dip." She glances at my swim trunks. "I guess you had the same idea."

"Yeah, let's go. I'll race you." Without waiting for her, I rush for the sand and into the sea. I don't want her to spend too much time staring at me or she will see my reaction to her in my shorts.

The ocean is neither hot nor cold. It's just the right temperature to cool me down. Unfortunately, when I emerge from a rather brisk swim out, I find I have a company.

Lyric.

"The water feels amazing." She lifts her legs from underneath her and floats in the water. She's looking up at the sky with her sunglasses on while I tread and admire the beautiful buffet in front of me. "I'm so glad my friends gave me this trip. I really needed it."

"Working too hard at home?" I inquire.

She glances over at me. "Yeah, something like that."

I don't push for more. From the outset, when she agreed to share the villa, I promised to give her space, and that's what I'll do. We are both on vacation. We're supposed to leave our worries and stressors from home at the door. I determine to do that, live in the moment. I join her by floating on my back, too.

"This really is paradise," she says dreamily.

"The kind I can get used to," I respond.

"I thought Barbados was amazing," Lyric said, "but this is a close second."

"How was Barbados? I've never been."

"The beaches are much like here, pristine, soft sand and water so clear you can see your feet. I went there on a girls' trip."

"But you came here by yourself?"

She tucks her feet under her and looks at me. "Yeah, I did. As did you. Guess we both needed to get away from our lives back home."

"You have no idea."

I love Kianna and totally miss her. As a parent, I always put her first. But when Chantel suggested this trip, I knew she was right. I *needed* some time to myself, to consider my own needs. My desires. Especially since this is the anniversary of my divorce. I can't help but remember the hopes I had for the future, when we first got engaged, or our failure to live up to the promises we made.

Maybe Chantel is right. Maybe it's time to bury the past and start anew. Maybe even forgive myself.

"Care to tell me about it?" she inquires. Her eyes search

mine and when I don't expound, she adds, "If it's too personal, you don't have to talk about it."

"Suffice it to say, I have some demons I need to deal with and I'm hoping to bury them so I can move on with my life."

Lyric nods. "I understand. I have a lot on my plate when I get back home to Memphis, too. This week is all about allowing myself some fun and letting go. Perhaps you could do the same?"

"With you?"

Her gaze is drawn to my mouth and she flicks out the tip of her tongue and dampens her lips. "Maybe." I follow her movements, and when she glances up, there's a flash of heat in her eyes as she realizes I'm watching her.

A flame of excitement shoots through me. The pure, unadulterated chemistry zigzagging between us is potent. It does something strange to my senses.

And it isn't one-sided. Her expression is confirmation of that.

"Do you want me to kiss you?" My voice rumbles in my chest, and I can feel my heart thumping loudly as I wait for her to reply.

Her answer is to swim closer. Her word is a whisper, but it's all I need.

"Yes."

My arms wrap around her slender waist, and I dip my head to settle my lips over hers. Her lips part beneath mine and a sense of triumph fills me because she kisses me back with a hunger that matches my own. I tangle one hand in her hair and pull her slick body against mine so her pelvis is pressed against my aching dick.

Is she shaking or is that me?

I can't tell because I'm lost in her response. So I kiss her again, and again.

Any control I've ever had is gone. In its stead is a desperate need to have her.

Three

Lyric

Am I really kissing a stranger I just met hours ago as if my life depends on it?

Yes, I am.

My arms wrap around his neck as he kisses me slow and deep, with bone-shaking eroticism. I know he had to feel me shake.

I've never experienced this kind of attraction to anyone. It must be the same for him, because he's thrusting his tongue between my lips and boldly exploring my mouth like he can't get enough. I can feel a solid ridge between the thin barrier of swimsuits between us.

I want to be closer so I press my body to his. He groans. "Damn it, Lyric."

Then his hands are down my back. He's drawing the

straps of my bikini top down, baring my breasts. I feel the cool air against my wet skin.

"You are the most beautiful creature I've ever seen," he says hoarsely before bending his head to close his lips around one of my dark brown nipples.

My cry echoes across the waves as he sucks me into the warm cavern of his mouth. With each pull, I gasp at the sharp sensation.

"Devon," I sob.

I never knew my small breasts could be so acutely sensitive. His attention is already on the other breast as he swoops it into his mouth. I circle my legs around his waist, pressing his dick against where I ache.

He senses what I need and one of his hands goes lower in the water. I feel him push aside the wet fabric of my bikini bottoms. I'm tipped off-balance yet again when he explores the seam of my vulva, parting my folds, his fingers thrusting inside me.

A low, keening cry releases from my chest as he invades me with his fingers. "I want to kiss you again," I whisper, and he obliges, kissing his way up from my breasts to my throat to my mouth.

I tighten my arms around his neck and thrust my tongue into his mouth, trying to tell him without words how badly I need this.

His fingers grow insistent. "Do you like that?" he asks, his voice thick as he pushes a third finger into me, swirling them in an erotic dance.

My answer is to arch my hips and move against his hand. When the flutters of my orgasm strike, my internal muscles clench around his fingers. Another sob of abandon escapes. He crushes my lips to his as I break and fly apart.

My orgasm is so powerful I don't realize Devon is carrying me back to the beach with my legs still wrapped tightly around his waist. When he reaches the steps of the villa, he sits down on the one of the recliners, with me still straddling him, until I finally come back to myself. I'm trembling and weak and vaguely aware of Devon tying the knot at the nape of my neck to put my bikini back in place.

Suddenly, I feel embarrassed. I'm sitting on a stranger's lap after allowing him to bring me to climax. But my embarrassment somehow only makes me want to get closer. I lower my head and nuzzle his neck.

In my everyday life, I keep men at a distance because I've always felt awkward, unsure. The few times I've been intimate, I held back and couldn't always orgasm. Sometimes, I faked it.

I've never felt as if I was particularly sexy. My body has always been a vessel for ballet. I honed it to fit that ideal. Small hips and breasts are common in the industry, so I've always been self-conscious about my curves. Yet in this moment, Devon has made me feel sexier and wilder than I've ever felt. He seems to like my body just as it is.

His hands rub my back slowly. "It's okay, Lyric," he murmurs, "there's nothing to be embarrassed about. We're two grown-ass adults."

I sigh and force myself to lift my head and look into his light brown eyes. He isn't looking at me with censure. In fact, he appears to be as astonished as I am by what just happened.

"I—that doesn't normally happen with me."

He frowns. "What do you mean?"

"It's just… I've never had such a powerful orgasm before."

"And I wasn't even inside you," Devon says. "Imagine how great *that* could be."

I blush yet again. I'm not used to talking about sex so openly. "I've had very limited experience in the bedroom."

"I see." Devon rubs his beard. "The passion we shared out there—it's unusual for me, too."

I'm relieved it's not just me.

"I think we need a moment to, uh, cool off. I damn near made love to you out in the ocean and I didn't even have protection with me," Devon says.

Protection.

I was so caught up in the moment, I would have let him fuck me out there without a condom, where anyone could have seen us. No wonder he's pulling away. He's using common sense while the intensity of what we shared has gotten me carried away.

I need to get my head straight. This trip is about a fresh start, about discovering who I am outside of professional ballet. About the risks I'm willing to take to start a new career, to finally welcome my future…and my past. And if my fresh start is going to include exploring my sexuality, then I'm going to have to be an adult and practice safe sex.

Slowly, I climb off his lap. Thought I want to rush to my room, he grasps my hips, not allowing me to move.

"Lyric, how about we go out for dinner at one of the resort restaurants? We can, uh, talk about what comes next."

I'm certain he's thinking about me in his bed, but I need time to collect myself. "Yes, that's fine."

"I'll meet you in the living room at 7:00 p.m."

"Okay."

I rush off to the primary bedroom Devon was kind enough to allow me to take, and I lock the door after me. I don't think he's going to come in. It's more to keep me away from him. *I'm* the one who acted on impulse.

How could I have behaved so completely out of character? I don't do random hookups. Of my last two relationships, one man was a white male dancer with whom I partnered. It seemed like a natural progression because we had the same passion for dance. The sex was good, but we didn't have much else in common. He didn't understand what it was like to be a Black woman in ballet.

He moved on to another ballerina after I broke up with him. To get back at me, he labeled me cold and the description stuck, hurting my self-confidence.

My other lover was one of the choreographers at a show I was doing. He was older than me, and I was completely infatuated with him. The sex was pleasant enough, but I often didn't feel relaxed enough to orgasm and faked it.

With Devon, however—he made feel beautiful and sexy and desired. He made me feel like I could own my sexuality, like the other Gems. Egypt is bold and proud to be a tall, sexy, full-figured woman. Asia has always had a style all her own that's audacious and sassy, just like the spitfire she is. Wynter is stacked like a brick house with curves for days and easily snagged Riley, Shay's brother.

Speaking of Shay, she's been messing around with an

old classmate of ours and getting her swerve on. And Lord knows what Teagan is up to. That woman has always known what she wants so I doubt she has any trouble telling a man exactly how to serve it up. That leaves me, Lyric, the quiet and reserved one in our group.

I've never really owned my femininity any more than I've owned being a Black woman. Being raised by two Caucasian parents—bless their hearts, they didn't know how to help me accept my ethnicity. They never denied that my heritage was different than theirs, but they didn't help me embrace it, either. They couldn't understand that what made me different wasn't just the color of my skin.

In school, I was the Black girl with nappy hair whose mother didn't know how to comb it. The best Mama could do was brush my curly strands and put them into a ponytail. However, as I grew older, I noticed other Black girls had straight hair. I wanted to look like them and like the blondes and brunettes in my class with silky hair down their backs. I had to explain it to Mama, who researched online and eventually began taking me to a Black hair salon. Once my hair was relaxed, I felt somewhat accepted by other kids in my class, but I was still the strange one with white parents.

When we moved to San Antonio for several years for my father's work, I begged my parents to put me into a public high school where more people looked like me. They agreed, and that's when I met the Gems. I loved my friends, but I rarely dated. The Black boys in high school didn't think I was Black enough even though I was surrounded by the Gems. They told me I talked white. What does that mean? I speak good English? Or they thought I dressed too preppy, like a white girl. I didn't understand how I couldn't be Black enough when my experience in ballet showed otherwise. Had they seen my skin in the summertime? My normal café au lait skin turns the color of chestnut.

My past makes me feel woefully out of my depth in this situation with Devon. My lack of sexual experience, coupled with my lack of knowledge about dating Black men, is a recipe for disaster. Maybe I should cut my losses and ask the manager to put me in another room…

I glance at the clock.

Is it really six o'clock?

Shit!

If I don't meet him in the living room, he'll think I'm afraid to face him and that's more humiliating than Devon knowing of my sexual inadequacies.

Rushing into the bathroom, I turn on the taps and climb inside the shower. It's blessedly hot and it washes away some of the salt water and sand leftover from my heated moment. Afterward I moisturize my skin with my favorite perfumed lotion, straighten my shoulder-length auburn hair and add a bit of makeup to give me some color. I walk into the living room with just minutes to spare.

Devon is already there, looking devilishly handsome in a pair of linen pants and a white button-down shirt. Why does he have to look so damn hot?

He smiles as I walk down the corridor, and it gives me a bolt of confidence. I'm wearing a plunging maxi dress with a knot in the center of the bust that gives me the look of cleavage. I've never been more than an A cup. In ballet it's all about being thin. Most of the women are flat-chested with not a hint of body fat. Once, my dance company in-formed me that my breasts, small as they are, would be con-sidered a distraction to members of the audience. They told me to lose weight. I did, but the breasts remained.

"You look stunning," Devon says when I reach him. He takes my hand and brings it to his lips.

I smile. "Thank you."

"I took the liberty of calling us a ride." Devon opens the villa's double doors.

Sure enough, a golf cart is waiting and whisks us off to the resort's popular seafood restaurant. It's right on the beach, so I take off my shoes and walk in the sand. It's soft and powdery. The hostess seats us at a table with an ocean view and leaves us with the wine selection.

"I can't believe I'm here," I say.

"The view is one of the reasons I chose this resort. I wanted someplace with a killer beach and a restaurant with an extensive array of foods," Devon responds. He's not look-ing at the menu, but instead he stares at me as if *I'm* on the menu.

"What looks good?"

I'm determined to get back on an even keel, but he's not making it easy. I'm appreciative when the waiter comes over and makes a production out of the wine list. After Devon and I taste our selections, we eventually settle on a sauvi-gnon blanc. It's crisp and delicious with a slight taste of apple. I take a sip and wait for what's coming next. Devon wastes no time getting right down to business.

"I thought it was good idea to get away from the villa. Things got pretty intense out there in the ocean."

I nod. Afraid to speak, I let him continue.

"I want you to know I didn't suggest us sharing the villa as a way to get into your pants."

His unexpected comment makes me laugh. "I never thought that."

An audible sigh of relief escapes his lips. His bottom lip is slightly fuller than the top and it makes me want to suck it into my mouth.

Focus, Lyric. Focus.

"Good, I'm glad," Devon said, "but I would be lying if I said I wasn't attracted to you from the start, Lyric. I noticed you on the plane earlier today. Are you from Memphis, too?"

"I am. And I didn't pick up on your interest." A total lie, but I'm not ready to admit it yet. I like flirting.

He cocks his head as if he doesn't believe me. "I was checking you out and you were doing the same thing to me." When I start to open my mouth, he interrupts, "Don't even try to deny it."

I shrug. "Okay, I admit I thought you were hot."

A broad smile lights up his face. "You did?"

"Don't go getting a big head or anything. You know you're good-looking."

"And you're not?"

I shrug. "I've been told I'm too skinny or—" I use quotation marks "—'too slender,' nothing for a man to hold on to."

"Oh, I held on," Devon said with a smirk.

My mind recalls him cradling my ass against his rock-hard erection. Color rises and blooms in my cheeks.

"I like how in this day and age, there's a woman like you who can still blush at something a little naughty."

I laugh wryly. "Yes, I believe we were a bit naughty today."

"We were, and I'd like a lot more," Devon responds. "Just not with any audience."

"You would?"

I'm surprised. I thought I might be too inexperienced for a man like Devon, who I'm certain has had a lot more sex than I have. He was married, after all. My couple of intimate relationships didn't last very long because I was wary of getting involved. I had my career to look forward to, but now that I'm no longer onstage I don't want to be afraid of exploring new things.

"Don't act so surprised, Lyric. I know the attraction is mutual. The connection we shared today was off the charts. I would like to explore that for long as we're here."

"You mean what happens in Aruba, stays in Aruba?"

He points to me. "Exactly! What do you say?"

Four

Devon

*P*lease say yes.

Please say yes.

I wait patiently for Lyric's answer when I all I want to do is clear off the table and eat her for dinner and dessert. If this afternoon was a taste of the powerful chemistry between us, then I want the entire buffet. And judging from her expression, I'm confident I'll get it.

I search her face with lustful eyes, then reach across the table and twine our hands together. Hers are soft, small in comparison to mine. I can feel her pulse beating in rapid succession. Lyric's lashes flutter closed.

"Why are you hesitating?"

Her eyes fly open to regard me. "I don't usually do this."

"Have vacation flings?"

Once again, her blush rises from her chest and goes up

to her cheeks. I love the physical signs that she's hot and bothered, out of her comfort zone.

"I think you and I could be a dangerous combination," she responds.

"Which will make it even more fun."

I watch as she squirms in her seat. She wants me, but she's afraid to go after it. My eyes travel down her face to her neck and lower to her breasts. I see the outline of her nipples in the maxi dress she's wearing.

"Your nipples are hard for me," I say, and watch her eyes widen as she stares at me open-mouthed. I continue to tease. "I bet your panties are wet for me right now, should I try to feel for myself?" We are seated close enough that her leg is touching mine, if I slid my hand down a touch to the left...

She vigorously shakes her head.

"No?" I ask with a smile. "Make no mistake about how much I want you, Lyric, and I know you want me, too. Take what you want. Let the fire that started hours ago incinerate us both."

She reaches for her drink and takes a languorous sip. My entire body tightens as I await her answer. When she glances up, there's a flame burning there. Her gaze never leaves my face as she mulls over her response. Then she inhales sharply, which tells me I have her.

"All right, for this week only."

I nod. "Just this week. I can't offer you anything beyond that anyway."

"Understood."

A satisfied smile curves my lips. Dinner will be delicious, I'm sure, but I can't wait for dessert.

★ ★ ★

To ease Lyric's nerves about how the evening will end, I engage her in conversation after we order our entrees. Lyric opts for the branzino with potato puree and lemon caper jus while I go for the sea scallops with Parmesan risotto and citrus vinaigrette. We share a few pertinent facts about ourselves, but don't go too deep.

I don't want to talk about my past, my deceased ex-wife or my daughter. I'd like this week to be about the two of us, this attraction we've had for each other since the moment we laid eyes on each other, and nothing more. We can leave our pasts at the door.

"You know, I have no idea how old you are."

"Does it matter?" she asks.

"No, I was just curious."

"I'm thirty," Lyric responds.

"And I'm thirty-two. Our ages match up perfectly. What about family? Any brothers or sisters?"

Lyric shakes her head. "No, I'm an only child. I was adopted."

"You were? When did you find out?"

"When I was five years old. My parents were completely transparent, but it wasn't always easy being different from other kids. How about you?"

"My parents are divorced," Devon says. "It was acrimonious, but my sister and I try to remain neutral, but it's not easy." To keep from getting too much into our personal lives, I pivot. "If you don't mind my asking, what do you do for a living?"

"I run my own business." She doesn't tell me what kind

of business. If she wants to keep a layer of anonymity between us, that's fine with me. It will make it easier when we go back to Memphis.

"That sounds intriguing. How long have you had it?"

"It's a new development. I've actually been working for other companies my entire life. It's nice to have something that's mine. Something I can call my own."

"Congratulations. I can't imagine it's easy being a business owner."

She shakes her head. "It isn't. All the responsibility falls to me, but I'm up for the challenge. I had a guardian angel and was blessed with a small inheritance that helped me get my company off the ground. And what about you? What's your calling?"

"I'm a software engineer. I design, develop, test and debug software to ensure it meets our customers' needs and performs optimally. It's a computer job, but I love it and it happens to pay the bills."

"Doing what you love is important," Lyric replies. "I had that once, but I was injured and unable to pursue my life's passion."

"That stinks. How did you overcome it?"

"By finding a new dream, and that's opening up my own business."

"Good for you. Adversity builds character."

Her eyebrow rises a fraction, "Sounds like you know something about that."

"I do," I respond. "When my ex-wife passed, I was left to pick up the pieces and take care of our daughter."

"You have a child?" Shock is evident in her voice.

Damn it, I hadn't intended to mention Kianna at all, but I guess I'm so comfortable with her, I let it slip. I'm silent for a few moments as I figure out exactly what I want to say. Kianna is important to me. And Lyric has to understand this week is all I have to give.

"I do."

"I see."

I don't like Lyric's careful tone. "I wasn't trying to keep her a secret, but I'm very protective of her. She's the best thing that ever happened to me."

"Said like a proud father," Lyric replies with a grin, and it makes me smile that she understands and gives me some slack.

"Has it been difficult being a single parent?"

I nod. "It has, but Black women do this all the time and they don't complain, so why should I?"

Lyric laughs. "I like you, Devon. Not many people give single mothers the credit they deserve."

"I call it how I see it. Would you be upset if I called an end to dinner and suggested we have our dessert back at the villa?"

Her smile turns coy. "Are you trying to get back so you can have your wicked way with me?"

"Abso-fucking-lutely!"

We both laugh, and I signal the waiter so I can take care of the bill, but only after we order desserts of crème brûlée with fresh berries and a chocolate torte cake with spiced almonds. When our desserts arrive in a bag, I eagerly stand to my feet. I can't wait to get Lyric back to the villa. I'm hungry for something else entirely and it ain't food.

The ride back in the golf cart is interminably slow. Lyric's scent fills my nostrils, and I find I can't think straight. There is a wild heat between us that defies reason or logic. Maybe it's finally having time to myself, or maybe it's knowing this has an expiration date, or maybe it's Lyric—but it's unlike anything I've ever felt.

My sole focus is Lyric and how I'm going to make love to her in every way imaginable. This week, I'll sate myself with her and when we're done, we can go our separate ways.

When we arrive at the villa, I put the desserts in the fridge and turn to find Lyric in the living room, waiting for me. Without hesitating, I walk to her and pull her into my arms. Her slender curves fit perfectly against my hard body. I seek her mouth, and she capitulates, parting her lips for me. The maelstrom of desire that tormented me in the sea earlier returns full force, crashing over us.

Without taking my mouth off hers, I lift Lyric into my arms and carry her toward her bedroom. It doesn't matter which bedroom we use because, before this week is week is over, I intend to have her in every room.

I set Lyric on her feet at the foot of the king-size bed and reach behind her to unzip her dress. Slowly, I draw the material away from her lithe body, revealing her to my appreciative gaze. She is swathed in lacy underwear. Her bra is sheer enough I can see the nipples I sucked earlier, and that I intend to gorge on again now with no interruption. A tiny pair of lace panties barely covers her mound, and I can't wait to have a taste.

Rocking back on my knees, I simply look my fill. Soon,

she'll be naked and writhing underneath me. I begin to strip, unbuttoning my shirt. My shoes and socks are next, which allows me to step out of my trousers with quick efficiency. I'm desperate to be inside her, but I don't want to come on too strong. Lyric said she's new to this. She has no idea she is my dream girl come to life.

She's even more so when she reaches behind her to unfasten her bra, allowing it to fall to the floor. Her beautiful, creamy café au lait breasts with dark brown tips call out to me like some sort of siren's song. And when she hooks her fingers into her panties and tugs them down her legs to stand in front of me in nothing but her high heels, I nearly come right then and there. But I want our first time to be good, so I'm going to control my impulse to quickly bury myself inside her.

Lyric surprises me by walking over and pulling down my boxers. My dick—thick, long and hard—springs free from the mass of black hairs growing at its base. Her eyes grow large at seeing how big I am. She's quite slender, so when the time comes, I'll have to make sure she's ready for me.

Walking her backward, we fall to the bed, and I move in to kiss her. I coax her lips apart with my tongue so I can explore her sweetness. She tastes so damn good. Our mouths come together in a passionate duel as the kiss goes on and on. By the time I lift my head, I have to drag air into my lungs and I can feel Lyric shaking underneath me at the intensity of our desire.

"It's okay," I whisper. "I've got you."

I intend to worship and revere her. Let her know her body is beautiful just as she is. I've picked up on hints that she's self-conscious and she shouldn't be. So I take my time, trailing my lips over her throat, nuzzling, licking and sucking as I go. When I reach her puckered nipples, I draw one hard nub in my mouth and suck. She lets out a choked sound that makes the beast in me come to life.

I allow myself this moment because all we have is this week.

I continue my sensual torture on her other breast while my hands skim lower to her flat stomach and beyond to the vee of curls between her thighs. When I ease her legs apart, a tremor runs through her, especially when I rub my fingers over her slick heat and part her folds. I slide one finger, then two, inside her as I did earlier, applying the right amount of pressure with my thumb to her sensitive nub.

"Oh!" She shudders and begins to ride my hand, her fingers clutching at the sheets. But I don't want her to come by my touch. I want to taste her. A soft moan of protest escapes her lips when I withdraw my fingers, but when I lower myself past her breasts and stomach to nudge her thighs apart with my shoulders, Lyric tenses.

"It's okay." I soothe her with my hand. Then I'm parting the swollen outer lips to push my tongue between them and discover her sticky wetness.

"Devon!"

Lyric comes apart and I delight in the sounds of her husky moans as I pleasure her with my mouth. She tastes like the nectar of the gods. When she tries to push me away, I don't let her; I use my tongue to bring her to a second orgasm.

"Now, please..."

She pulls me up toward her damp body. I pause long

enough to reach for the condoms in my trousers. They were a last-minute purchase, but I'm so glad I had the foresight to bring them. I quickly sheath myself with protection while she looks up at me with wonder in her eyes.

I can't resist the pull to be inside her and move my hands under her bottom to lift her toward me. I lock eyes with hers and rub my thick, swollen dick up and down her moist opening.

She's ready for me, all right.

"Do you want this?" I ask.

I know she does, but I need to hear her confirmation.

"Yes, yes!"

Five

Lyric

I plead and beg for Devon to fuck me and he does. He eases forward and penetrates me with one deep, powerful thrust. A shocked gasp escapes my lips as I accept the awesome length of his dick. My vaginal muscles quickly stretch to accommodate him, but he's not moving. I can feel him pulsing inside me as he gives me time.

His hands settle on my hips and he begins to move. He establishes a rhythm with steady strokes, and I move my hips against his, desperate for him to pick up the pace.

Once again, just like in the ocean, I'm a wanton creature, clutching him, raking my nails over his back as he claims me with every stroke. His hardness against my softness. I cradle his face in my hands and suck on his tongue as pressure builds inside me.

His hips move harder and faster, and I can't hold on. I

let out a helpless cry when one thrust hits all my sensitized nerve endings. I didn't know it was possible my body could explode with pleasure, but that's what it feels like. I sob his name as he sends me over the edge. I'm free-falling, but Devon doesn't stop. He lifts my backside and pumps into me, making my orgasm go on and on.

I can see the corded muscles of his neck and his shoulders straining as he throws his head back and releases a roar before collapsing on top of me.

It's everything I didn't know I was missing out on.

Devon soothed away my old fears, my insecurities about my body. Now that I've had a taste of this pleasure, of what it means to feel beautiful and sexy, I want more.

I have all week to take it.

Eventually, Devon rolls away from me and disposes of the condom, but he's soon back in bed beside me. I thought he was going to his room. Instead, he pulls me to him, spooning me. My backside nestles into his crotch.

"How about we forgo our individual bedrooms?" Devon asks, his mouth trailing a path of wet kisses down my neck. "Would that work for you?"

I nod because I'm pretty much spent after that incredible lovemaking session. No other experience has prepared me for what we just shared. I've done the physical act with two other men, but it's been a long time, and I don't remember ever feeling this way.

It's like Devon has awakened my body from a long slumber.

It's like he's awakened *me* from a long slumber.

I spent my life working, sacrificing, to become the next

Misty Copeland. I wanted to be a professional ballerina just like her, but I had no idea being African American would make it so hard. I had no idea how much work it would be.

I fell in love with ballet after Mama took me to a recital when I was five years old. Dance class was fun and magical, and I got to wear an adorable pink tutu. I loved twirling around and floating through the air.

I saw the way other students, and even their parents, looked at me. They were unsure what to make of me. With my fair skin and dark brown eyes, it was hard to tell what ethnicity I was. Was I Black or white like my adoptive parents, Brad and Ashley Taylor?

Back then, I didn't understand. Race didn't matter to me; I just wanted to dance.

I worked my ass off with endless trainings, rehearsals and competitions, all in my quest to become a principal dancer in a classical ballet company. I was really good, too, or so my Russian instructor, Aleksandr Smirnov, told me. He said I had promise and could be one of the rare few to have a professional career in dance.

With his guidance I went to the Youth America Grand Prix, where I received a scholarship from Juilliard. After graduation, I became a principal dancer with the San Francisco Ballet company.

It was a dream fulfilled. Yes, at a cost to my social life, my sensual life. But all the work was worth it when I was on the stage.

Then one night my foot caught in the hem of my dress, and I tripped in front of thousands of spectators at the War Memorial Opera House. I ruptured my Achilles tendon.

Although my feet were on the stage, I had the sensation I was in the air. I lost my hearing and peripheral vision for a moment and went into shock.

The surgery and recovery were grueling. I endured months of physical therapy, devastated at what I had lost. Ballet was my world. It was what I had worked my entire life to achieve. To have it taken away in the blink of an eye was heartbreaking.

To endure all I had, only to have an injury end my promising career...

I was a seasoned dancer and used to injuries. It was the indignity of working so long and so hard toward a goal only to have it all come crashing down within seconds.

So I made a new goal.

The Gems, namely Teagan, helped me realize I could put my dance background to good use. I didn't have to give up something I loved just because professional dancing was out of the picture. Teagan suggested teaching. I could find joy in helping other young dancers become better than they ever imagined. Opening a dance studio will allow me to enjoy the art of ballet even though I can no longer be onstage.

Even though I'm ready for this new dream, I miss performing in front of crowds and floating across the stage. I miss the applause. I miss doing what I was born to do.

I grieve for what once was, what could have been.

But tonight, the grief is not as sharp. And that's thanks to Devon.

I'm excited about spending the week with him and exploring the sensual nature I have too often ignored. In less than twenty-four hours, Devon has made me feel safe and secure enough to let go.

I've always had to stay focused, be in control of my body, my thoughts, my actions and how they could reflect on me, my parents, the ballet company. But right now, this week, it's just about me, about what I want. I fucking love it!

The next time I wake up, it's morning, but the pillow beside me is empty. I slip on one of the resort robes and go in search of Devon. He's in the kitchen, bare-chested, setting up a tray of breakfast.

I give him a shy smile. "What's all that?"

"I took the liberty of ordering in. I figured you would be exhausted after last night's festivities. I was about to bring you breakfast in bed."

I'm tired and a bit sore in some intimate areas, but in a good way. My sex life has never been particularly active so I'm going to need to soak in the Jacuzzi outside.

"Thank you." I pad over to see what's on the tray. There's bacon, eggs, pancakes, an omelet, fresh fruit, yogurt with granola, coffee, orange juice, and a variety of pastries. "Did you order everything on the menu?"

"Nearly. I wasn't sure what you liked."

I blush. We haven't exactly done a lot of talking other than the formalities about our careers and families. I don't even know how he takes his coffee, yet I went to bed with the man and had the most amazing sexual experience of my life. Ordinarily, I would want to know more about someone I'm intimate with, but I don't know, I feel different somehow. Free. Lighter. Without the baggage of my past pulling me down.

I'm experimenting and going with what feels good rather than what's customary or expected. I'm usually so reserved and focused. Yes, I expected this to be a solo vacation for self-reflection and looking ahead, but it feels good to explore this new side to myself.

"The omelet, fruit and granola work for me." I'm used to watching what I eat. It comes naturally after so many years of training to become a ballerina. Though I can't resist one piece of bacon and begin munching on it. I remember a time I wouldn't have been caught dead eating something so fatty.

"All right, I'll eat the bacon, eggs and pancakes. I'm starved." Devon takes the tray and we make our way back to the bedroom to enjoy the food. He tucks into his breakfast with gusto.

"You worked up quite an appetite. Are you always this, um, active?"

He laughs and stops midway to putting bacon in his mouth. "Are you saying you're not up to the task?"

I shake my head. "I didn't say that, but you do have a rather..."

"Voracious appetite?" he offers.

"Yes." I nod and reach for a coffee mug. The caffeine is an instant boost to my system.

"Not usually," Devon responds, "but I have to admit you and I suit each other."

I blush again. "Yes, we do."

I've felt desire before, but there's something different about Devon. I never clutched at their backs or moaned their

names. Devon's brand of sex is earthy, physical and demanding, *very demanding*. His hungry kisses unleash something I
hadn't known was hidden.

"So tell me, Lyric. How does a woman as beautiful as
you have such limited experience?" Devon inquires after
he's finished off his pancakes.

I keep my answer vague. This week is about enjoying
myself and nothing more. "Most of my childhood was spent
training for that dream, which I achieved. But it cost me, ya
know? I didn't always have time to spend chasing boys and…
well, I was behind my peers. That's not to say I didn't eventually venture out, but when I did, I found sex was fine."

Devon raises a brow. "Then you definitely weren't doing
it right. Or weren't with the right person. Sex should be an
enjoyable experience of giving and receiving."

"You appear very knowledgeable on the topic." I take
a few bites of my yogurt and granola and lower my head,
acting as if the holy grail can be found in the cup's depths.

"I've had my share, but I'm by no means a man-whore
if that's what you're saying."

I chuckle. "A man-whore?"

"Yeah." Devon laughs along with me. "You know, a
fuckboy who will lead you on with no intention of being
in a relationship. As soon as they get what they want, they
dump you and move on to the next girl."

"Wow! And how do you know so much about them?"

"It's sad to say, but I had a few friends like that in college
before I met my ex-wife. A couple of them have matured,
but there's one who lives to be a player. I know you're probably thinking birds of a feather, but I've never aspired to be

one of them. I like being in a relationship, or rather I used to before…" He stops his words as if he's said too much.

I wonder what he'd been about to say, but he rises from the bed. "You all finished?" he asks, glancing down at the tray, which is damn near empty.

Previously, I wouldn't have dreamed of eating my entire plate. All I would allow myself is maybe some egg whites for protein, because I was performing and knew my every move would be critiqued. Now, however, I'm free to let go of the restraints. I can allow myself to enjoy food and now, apparently, sex.

I nod. "Yes, thank you." I want to push him to finish our conversation, but I don't. A vacation fling is supposed to be fun, light and flirty, not dredging up past hurts. "How do you feel about exploring the town?"

"Sounds like fun," Devon says. "Let's do it."

While he finishes up with the tray, I hop off the bed and head to the closet. I unpacked all my clothes yesterday because I hate to have wrinkles. I search through my items until I find a strapless maxi dress with leaves all over. I team it with a belt, flat sandals and a few bangles.

After brushing my teeth, I move into the shower and allow the warm spray of the rain head to fall over my skin. The invigorating shower revives me. It's as if all my senses have been opened, *heightened*, and it all started with Devon.

Somehow, I'm still having trouble accepting that a man like Devon finds me attractive. I never thought I was pretty enough or sexy enough because I was always told to stay skinny. *Watch what you eat, Lyric. You need to lose weight, Lyric.*

It's no wonder I have a complex about my body, but Devon seems to like me well enough.

I don't know if I've conjured him up, but suddenly I sense his presence in the bathroom. His brown eyes rake over me and he inclines his head to the door, asking to join me.

I've never showered with a man and feel a bit self-conscious, but maybe this week is about breaking down my barriers. So I open the door and let him in. He takes the sponge from my hand, pours soap onto it and starts lathering every inch of my body. My breath catches in my throat as he strokes his way from my shoulder to my breasts. He pays special attention to them before sliding to my stomach and thighs. A hiss escapes my lips as he swipes over my buttocks and then moves his hand to the front and slips the sponge between my legs.

"Devon…" I glance up at him.

"Hmm…" He smiles down at me with a wicked grin as he dispenses with the sponge and slides one finger inside me, stretching me.

I fall backward against the cool tiles and let his fingers work their magic—in and out and in again in a slow, steady rhythm. I clutch his biceps, needing something to hold on to as he continues his assault. My internal muscles clench around his fingers. I close my eyes and allow the pleasure to take over, crying out as my orgasm hits me. Boneless, I lay back against the wall. When I finally gather my wits and open my eyes, Devon is showering as if he hadn't just brought me to a spectacular climax.

I want to do the same thing for him but am still working myself up to feel more confident with my sexuality. This week is about redefining myself and being brave enough to try new things. I suspect by the time it's over, I'll have conquered my insecurities. Maybe then I'll be ready to tackle bigger risks, like opening the studio and finally being ready to make contact with my biological mother.

Six

Devon

Damn, that was good. I'm still thinking about making Lyric come as I dress in a T-shirt and shorts for our day exploring Aruba.

I love how responsive she is to my touch, the heavy-lidded look in her eyes. Her taste on my tongue, the way my dick felt deep inside her last night.

When I booked this trip, I hadn't thought about hooking up with anyone, but on the off chance I might, I threw in a box of condoms. I'm glad I did, but I'm going to need a lot more with Lyric in my bed all week.

I walk out of the second bedroom and find Lyric in the living room. She's dressed in a strapless concoction that flows easily down her slender figure. I suspect she might have some hang-ups about her body, but by the end of this week, I'll make sure I've pushed aside every single doubt. She is everything I want in this moment.

I offer my hand. "Let's go."

This time, Lyric called for the golf cart, and it whisks us to the resort lobby where we take a taxi into the capital of Aruba, Oranjestad.

"It's beautiful here," Lyric says when we're dropped off in the downtown area.

"It is. I'm thankful it's not a big cruise day," I reply. The terminal is located in the port with only one ship in attendance. "I can only imagine how busy it gets if there's more than one boat in town. C'mon." I grab her hand and start walking down the cobblestoned streets.

It's a sunny day with hardly a cloud in the sky. I'm with a gorgeous, sexy woman, so I intend to enjoy it. We end up on a trolley car on Main Street with the driver narrating and giving us history about the island. We make a pit stop at the California lighthouse and climb the steps. It offers a view of the picturesque coastline. Once back on board the trolley, the driver regales us with details about the natural rock formations and giant boulders on Aruba's coast. Lyric and I decide we'll do a half-day trip there later in the week.

Slowly, the trolley makes its way back down Main Street, which is a vibrant thoroughfare of activity, lined with colorful buildings and boutique shops. Lyric mentions she wants to go shopping later and scoots closer to me.

Being with Lyric reminds me of how much I like being with someone who isn't afraid to show affection. Shiloh hated PDA and we rarely touched, let alone kissed, in public. I've always been a deeply physical man because that's my love language. Shiloh always told me I was too intense, too needy, so I tried to contain myself, to be the kind of husband she wanted. In the end, my restraint didn't help. Her career was always more important than me or our family.

Sometimes, I wonder if she ever loved me. Lyric catches my attention by pointing out the vibrant architecture, and I'm happy to be distracted from thoughts of my past. It's dangerous to think of Shiloh because it makes me remember all the things I did wrong, all the ways I failed in my marriage. The memories put me in a negative headspace, and I don't want that. I came to Aruba to get to a point of forgiveness and peace.

Maybe Lyric is the distraction that will help me get there.

Eventually, we disembark and stroll hand in hand down the promenade, weaving in and out of different souvenir shops hugging the marina. We find a variety of items geared toward tourists from T-shirts to hats to magnets to shot glasses and mugs. Lyric has to go in damn near every one of the stores even though they all have the exact same thing. We stop by some street vendors selling a range of local products and crafts. She decides on a tropical sundress along with a few T-shirts, magnets, key chains and some aloe vera products for her family and friends.

After a bit, we find ourselves at an open-air bar for a margarita. I have an El Jefe while Lyric settles on a passion fruit margarita and we nibble on some *pastechi*. We try an assortment of the deep-fried pastry pockets filled with cheese, ham, beef and chicken.

"What made you decide to come to Aruba?" Lyric asks, sipping her drink.

Yahrah St. John

I shrug. "I knew I wanted to go somewhere tropical, but I didn't want to go to one of the usual suspects like the Bahamas, Jamaica or DR. I wanted someplace different, off the beaten path, with great beaches. Aruba was the logical choice. Did you know Aruba is considered a desert?"

She laughs. "No, I didn't. Did you research that when you were trying to figure out where to go?"

"Maybe." I smile. "I can be a bit of a nerd sometimes. I like facts and learning new things."

"That's not a bad thing. What else do you like?"

"I like you," I respond unapologetically. I don't bother disguising my feelings. This affair won't last past the week. I can be as free and open as I want with no repercussions. I don't have to worry about the mistakes of the past, about being *too much,* too needy, too passionate like I was with my ex-wife. Besides, Lyric isn't running away from me. She's leaning toward me.

"I like you, too." She takes another sip of her drink.

Lyric is an open book. There's no artifice about her. How she feels shows directly on her face, on her light brown skin. She blushes easily, and I find it absolutely charming.

It's hard to detach from my emotions like I have done since my ex-wife died. The intensity of what I feel when I'm with her is disturbing. I'm used to being in complete control of myself, of not allowing a woman to get too close for fear of getting hurt or rejected. But right now, looking at Lyric, I'm fascinated. I don't have to pretend or restrain myself. This week, I can just be who I am.

"I don't seem to frighten you," I surprise myself by saying.

"Should I be frightened?" Lyric inquires.

"No, I've just been told I'm intense."

A spark glows suddenly in the depths of her brown eyes "You don't scare me, Devon."

I chuckle. I like the way Lyric looks at me. She's not afraid of a challenge. She can handle *all of me*. "That's good, Lyric, because this week I suspect I might surprise you."

She shrugged. "Bring it on."

It's well into the evening when we finally make it to the villa. Lyric falls asleep on the ride back and sleeps with her head on my shoulder. Her scent, a mix of vanilla and jasmine, fills my senses.

After I rouse her, I pay the driver and we walk up the path to the villa. Despite it being a warm night, it's breezy out. I'd read about Aruba's strong winds, but I had no idea it would be this windy, especially by the beach.

"How would you feel about getting in the hot tub?" I ask, once we're back inside and she's putting away the souvenirs she purchased.

"Sounds heavenly," she sighs. "My dogs are barking after all that walking. I could use some hydrotherapy."

"Excellent. I'll meet you back here in ten," I reply, and turn on the hot tub before heading to the second bedroom. I could easily bring my belongings to the primary bedroom, but I think it's good to have some boundaries.

During my marriage to Shiloh, I learned she liked to have her own space to do her own thing. Initially, it hurt because I assumed she didn't want to be with me. I was partially right. Shiloh loved me in her own way, but her craft always came before our marriage. I don't want Lyric to think I'm smothering her or vice versa. As long as we're sharing the same bed, that's all that matters to me.

A few minutes later, I emerge in my swim shorts. I head into the kitchen to find us libations. Looks like our refrigerator was refilled with another bottle of champagne. I'm popping off the top when Lyric comes sashaying in wearing a keyhole bikini top. It shows the swell of her small round breasts while the high-waisted bikini bottoms with sheer cutouts give her hips an added allure.

I feel like hanging my tongue out like a dog and panting, but I manage to keep it in my mouth, just barely, and return my focus to opening the champagne. There's a pop, and the cork flies across the room. Lyric bends over to pick it up, giving me a delicious view of her pert ass. Does she have any idea what she's doing to me?

I reach for two clean flutes on the open shelf and pour us each a glass. I offer her one and she accepts, taking a long sip.

"I could get used to this."

"So could I." But I'm not talking about the champagne.

If I had Lyric to come home to every night, I doubt I'd ever get any work done. Between her and Kianna, I'd have no time left. Kianna takes up most of my attention once I pick her up from Chantel's, where she goes after school. I'm thankful my family lives in Memphis and can help out. Some nights, Kianna stays with my parents, who, although twenty years older than me, are still youthful and love spending time with their granddaughter.

"Is the water hot yet?" Lyric inquires, staring longingly at the jets bubbling in the spa outside.

I glance down at the iPad that controls the lights, air-conditioning, shades and Jacuzzi. The villa has all the modern amenities. "Just," I say. "It might take a few more minutes."

"No problem." She puts a sheer cover-up over her swimsuit, hiding the view I've been enjoying. Then she goes out to the terrace with her flute and a towel. After spreading the towel on a lounger, she lies across it as if she were Aphrodite or something.

Rather than stare, I join her on the terrace, bringing the bottle of champagne with me. I top off her glass and mine and take the lounger beside her.

"This really is paradise," she says wistfully. "I didn't know how much I needed this. I guess the Gems knew."

"Gems?"

She turns to me with a wide smile. "It's the nickname for my girlfriends. We've had it for years, since high school."

"You still talk to friends you had from high school?"

She frowns. "Absolutely. Doesn't everyone?"

I laugh. "Not at all. I left them all behind when I went to college."

"I didn't," Lyric replies proudly. "These five women have gotten me through some dark days, and their friendship and our sisterhood means everything to me. I would trust them with my life."

The love she has for these women is evident. She cares for them deeply. "That's amazing, Lyric. The fact that you've been able to keep such strong bonds shows your character, loyalty and devotion. Those are hard to find these days."

She shrugs as if it's nothing, but it's not. I've had my share of relationships even before my marriage and can't recall a single person who spoke so passionately about friends or family.

"How did you come up with the name the Gems?"

A soft chuckle escapes her lips. "There's six of us," Lyric responds. "Teagan said boys would be lucky to date any of us. Asia said we were like the gemstones she uses in the jewelry she makes. We coined ourselves the Six Gems."

"You're certainly rare," I respond, looking into Lyric's almond-shaped eyes. For a moment, I wonder what it would be like if I could get to know her beyond this week and pull back the layers.

But it's not going to happen. I can't let it. I don't believe in love and commitment anymore. I used to believe in them, but found out it was all BS. All we have is this week, and when it's over we'll say our goodbyes.

"How about we get in that hot tub?"

Seven

Lyric

The way Devon had stared at me a moment ago was unnerving. It was like he could look into my very soul. He seemed touched by my relationship with the Gems, how we've fostered our sisterhood over the decades.

It hasn't always been easy.

After high school, we each went our separate ways. I was accepted into Juilliard while Wynter and Teagan both went off to college, Egypt to culinary school, Shay got married, and Asia followed her own path. But one thing was constant: our love for one another. We stayed in touch with video calls, texts, annual girls' trips and being present at major life events, and I'm proud of that.

Has Devon never known unconditional love like that? He appears skeptical that it's possible to be devoted and loyal to another person. *Did someone hurt him?* Is that why he's so guarded? He's the one who wanted what happens in Aruba to stay here. And I'm fine with it. I am.

However, if he asked me to reconsider when we got back to Memphis, I would be open to it. Last night was a revelation. I rather enjoyed exploring his body and can't wait to do so again tonight.

Eventually, the hot tub is warm enough and I remove my cover-up and slide down in the jetted water. I release an audible sigh. "This feels divine." Last night's intimacies have me aching in unfamiliar areas.

Devon is right beside me, following me into the water, but he's brought our flutes, topped off with more champagne.

"Are you trying to get me drunk?"

He laughs. "Yeah, is it working?"

"You're incorrigible!" I respond. "You don't have to try so hard. I think I showed last night I'm easy."

"Don't be so hard on yourself, Lyric. The attraction is mutual."

"I know. I just don't do casual affairs." I motion back and forth between us.

"Do you have regrets?"

"I'm here with you now. Does it look like I do?"

"And you're answering a question with a question," Devon responds, "but I'll take it."

I don't have any regrets because I'm here with Devon and exploring a side of myself I've never had time to explore before.

Don't get me wrong, I loved ballet and performing, but it sort of stunted my growth as a woman. It didn't allow me to experience things that other young girls and women my age did. And when I finally did have sex, it was pleasant, but not earth-shattering. I've *never* felt shattered like I felt last night.

I'm excited to have this week in Aruba. A time out of time, to see myself in a new light, as a complete woman able to enjoy life's pleasures.

If anyone can help me do that, it's Devon.

We spend the next several days in Aruba in the same vein as that second day on the island. A couple of them we spend on the beach, soaking up the sun's rays and snorkeling. My skin is now honey-kissed by the sun.

As for the rest of me, there's no part of me Devon hasn't touched, tasted, licked, teased or explored. He's discovered every hidden secret I've ever had and made me scream and cry out his name over and over again. One day, the villa became our love nest, and we didn't leave for twenty-four hours. We gorged on food, having breakfast, lunch and dinner brought to us via room service. We even ate in bed, with Devon feeding me. Other times, he used my body as a vessel for the food he licked off, covering me from head to toe until he had his fill.

As I lay on the beach reading a book and sipping a piña colada, I think about the trip so far. This week has changed me. I'm not the shy, insecure woman I was when I arrived. There's a new confidence; I'm feeling hella sexy. I've discovered I can express my needs and be in tune with a man's needs as well.

Just one look from Devon and my panties are wet. Yesterday, after exploring the rock formations by dune buggy, we went for lunch in town. Devon kept whispering how sexy I looked in my halter top and booty shorts, what he would like to do to me if we were alone. Somehow, I was convinced to go into the restroom of all places where Devon took me against the sink.

After donning a condom, he snatched down my shorts and drove into me. The friction of his body against mine made the flames catch. And when he opened his mouth against my neck and rolled his hips, the experience felt otherworldly. The sensual assault was so intense, I couldn't help but succumb. Convulsive waves shook me so hard, Devon had to put his hand over my mouth to cover my screams.

I'm capable of being wild, free, spontaneous and a little bit naughty. It feels good to shake off the shackles of the past. This week has made me feel stronger. Maybe I can use this newfound confidence in my everyday life to be bold, daring and willing to take a chance even if I don't like the result.

"Penny for your thoughts?" Devon asks from beside me on the lounger.

I cover. I don't want him to know how he's got me completely wide open. "What do you think about going out dancing tonight?"

"Dancing?" He frowns as if the word sounds distasteful.

"Yeah, it would be fun to see what sort of nightlife Aruba has."

"Um, sure, if that's what you want to do," Devon responds.

He doesn't sound very excited at the prospect, but I don't care. I'm learning to go for what I want. I haven't danced for fun in ages. It's always been about perfection and performance. Practicing day in and day out until my feet bled. Now it's time I lived a little and did something for the joy of it.

This whole week has been a joy. I *enjoy* spending time with Devon. We've gone to trivia night and karaoke at the resort. Devon has a surprising ability to know all things movies while I have a penchant for music. We were a good team and won free spa treatments, which we're using on our last day at the resort.

As for karaoke, listening to Devon belt out "Locked Out of Heaven" by Bruno Mars was one of the funniest things I've ever witnessed. I wasn't any better singing Gloria Gaynor's "I Will Survive," but it was a fun night. Neither one of us cared how bad we sounded.

There's a beauty in being solely myself with him. When I was in the dance world, I had to conform to a certain image, be reserved and classic so I fit in with the white, body-conscious industry. I was stifled and could only let my hair down when I was with the Gems or spending time with my family.

Devon allows me to be me.

After spending a couple more hours on the beach, we take an Uber back to the villa and get ready for our night out on the town. I brought a cocktail dress with me for such an occasion.

It's a simple black slip dress with an asymmetrical hem and a thigh-high slit in the front. It's both elegant and sassy. I pull my hair into a loose updo and leave a few tendrils out to frame my face. I'm not one for lots of makeup, so I add a little eyeliner, mascara and lipstick and my look is complete. Staring at myself in the mirror, I'm impressed with the reflection looking back at me.

Devon seems more than a little pleased, if the heated gaze he gives me is anything to go by. "Are you ready to paint the town red?"

"Absolutely, let's do it!"

A taxi picks us up and takes us to the Gusto. From my research online, it was voted the top bar in Aruba three years in a row for its trendy nightlife, international DJs and three dance levels.

When we arrive at 10:00 p.m. on Friday, the club is already buzzing with people milling about. We find a spot on the terrace outside, eager to enjoy the hot weather because when we get back to Memphis, it will be too frigid.

"What will you have?" the waitress asks once we find a table and sit down.

"I'll take a scorpion," I reply.

"A Bud Light for me," Devon responds.

I glance around the lively nightclub. "This place is a vibe."

"Yeah." Devon doesn't sound enthused. In fact, I would say he's bored with the surroundings.

I cock my head to one side to look at him. "I take it you don't go out much?"

"When I was younger, but now that I'm a father there's not much time for dance clubs."

I know he's a dad, but sometimes I forget about the responsibilities he has back home. I guess that's because we've kept our lives in Memphis private, only sharing pertinent facts as they come up, but not offering much else. I didn't elaborate about the dance studio I'm opening soon, even though LT Dance Academy is my pride and joy. With my parents' and the Gems' help, I got the studio ready for opening a couple of weeks early, allowing me this time to get away. I'm excited to share my love of dance with young students eager to learn about ballet, tap or jazz. I'm just not sure Devon would appreciate the outside world creeping into our time here so I've remained mum.

Right now, we're in a bubble, and I'd like to keep it that way. Here, I can give in to my every desire and enjoy my sexual liberation.

"Me either," I respond. "I'm usually too busy at work or spending time with family and friends. But upon occasion, I like to turn up with the Gems."

That brings a smile to his face. "So there's no one special?"

I shake my head. "Afraid not. And I certainly wouldn't be here with you if there were. Being with you has allowed me to be free. Freer than I've ever been."

"Same goes for me." A hot flames leaps into his eyes, and an emotion I can't name flickers across his handsome face.

"What is it? What's wrong?" My hand jerks out and touches his cheek.

"My past, the divorce, it affected me."

"How so?"

"I don't want speak ill of the dead, but my ex, she found me a bit much, so I tried to be less intense, softer and more palatable, because I wanted our marriage to work. But it *didn't* work. In the end there was nothing left but broken promises."

"I'm sorry, Devon. That's terrible. You should never be afraid to be who you are." I know I'm one to talk because I've conformed to fit the industry I've lived in all my life. "I hope you know that with me you can always be real and raw. I want it all."

Before I can say another word, Devon reaches for me and kisses me, hot and hungry, setting free something I suspect has been caged in him for a long time.

I don't even hear the waitress return with my fruity cocktail and his beer. All I can think about is how being with Devon is overwhelming, but also not nearly enough.

Eight

Devon

When we separate, our breathing is labored. Lyric's cheeks are flushed and her lips are red and full from my kisses. My heart thuds loudly in my chest.

I never imagined I'd meet a woman as sexy as Lyric on vacation. I came to Aruba to figure out how to get past my divorce and the failures in my marriage. So many things went wrong; I blame myself. Time and time again, my ex chose her career over me. It made me feel as if I wasn't enough. As if I wanted too much.

Because of her, I have only occasionally dated, and only those women who are safe, easygoing and fleeting. I love deeply and I never thought that was a bad thing until my marriage ended. Since then, I've vowed to never feel that way again, to never be heartbroken. Lyric, however, could make me reconsider.

It's a good thing I'm only allowing myself a week with her. Being with Lyric is dangerous for my equilibrium. If I'm not careful, she could be the one who tears down the walls I built around my heart after my marriage nearly destroyed me. I don't want to go through that again, but damn if she's not tempting me to want more.

"You ready to get out on the dance floor?" Lyric asks.

I know Lyric is excited to be here, but this really isn't my scene. It brings back memories of Shiloh. She loved to party, enjoyed being the center of attention while I liked staying in the background. I prefer my own company, which is why I booked this solo trip to begin with, but I can't deny the light shining in Lyric eyes. I would never want to dim that.

"If you insist," I respond underneath my breath, but she doesn't hear me because she's already heading into the club. I find her on the dance floor, jamming to a Beyoncé song. Her hands are in the air and her lithe body sways back and forth. She beckons me and I have no choice but to move forward as if she's a mermaid tempting me into the water.

I grab hold of her waist and pull her closer to me, away from several men who I notice can't keep their eyes off her any more than I can. She can dance. She feels the music and it flows through her body. I want to be here with her in this moment because it's all I can offer her. Having her in my arms feels right. Her skin is soft and her eyes are bright as she looks up at me with pure happiness.

I revel in it as I will revel in her later tonight. Our bodies sway to the music, and I lose myself in her. We stay on the floor for hours, caught up in the vibe and in each other.

Eventually, we take a break to catch our breaths and get another drink.

"That was fun," she says, out of breath, as I motion the bartender over.

I order another round. I can't recall the last time I had a good time dancing. Memories of arguments with Shiloh and how we could never see eye to eye haunt me. Reminding me of why I've kept women at arm's length and had fleeting dalliances. Because I don't want to endure that kind of heartache again. It broke me, made me question myself. I never want to feel that way again.

Instead, I focus on Lyric. Her forehead is damp with perspiration, which she blots with a napkin from the bar. When our drinks arrive, she nearly downs hers in one gulp.

"Easy, girl." I take the drink away from her. "That's not water or Kool-Aid. Those scorpions can sneak up on you."

She gives me a broad smile. "I can handle my liquor."

Famous last words.

Two hours later, I'm tucking her into bed at the villa. I'd hoped to bury myself inside her, but she kept throwing back the cocktails until she was a too tipsy to dance and I literally had to carry her outside. She doesn't protest when I unzip her dress, pull the fabric from her beautiful body and place it over a chair.

My heart beats erratically in my chest when I notice she's only wearing a thong. Sweet Jesus. I was hoping she had on some sort of fancy bra contraption. If I'd known she was bare underneath, we wouldn't have stayed long at the bar. It's for the best.

I pull the covers up over her nearly naked form and start

to disrobe, removing my shirt and trousers before joining her in bed. It'll be the first night we haven't made love since we arrived on the island. Despite her inebriation, Lyric senses me and curls toward me. I draw her into my arms. I stroke her silky hair with my hand and press a kiss to her forehead.

In another lifetime, Lyric could have been *my woman*, but we're in the here and now. When the incredible lovemaking is all we can have because I can't afford any emotional entanglements. The pain I felt after the failure of my marriage soured me on relationships entirely. My focus is my daughter.

I ignore the dull ache around my heart that has nothing to do with the amazing woman in my arms, close my eyes and drift off to sleep.

Nine

Lyric

As I look out over the ocean from the villa's kitchen window, it dawns on me that it's our last day on the island. I'm looking forward to it, yet I'm not. It'll be the last night I'll spend with Devon and I can't help but feel sad. As it is, I'm wearing his shirt. When I woke up, I found myself all but naked save for my thong. He undressed me and put me to bed.

Did I dream he held me to him last night and kissed my forehead? Is it possible he genuinely likes me? Does it matter? I have so much on my plate waiting for me when I get back home. I'm starting a brand-new business. A dance studio. I've never taught ballet before, but Aleksandr allowed me to come to his studio to watch him. Not to emulate, but to figure out my own style of teaching.

So I guess I'll never know what could have been with Devon. I smile ruefully to myself.

It doesn't matter. The passion we found here in Aruba gave me an awareness of myself and my sexuality that I've never had before. I just wish we had the chance to get to know each other better than we could during these seven days and seven nights.

"Can I have some of that?" Devon asks, inclining his head at the coffee mug I'm holding.

"Of course." I reach for a ceramic mug from the open shelf and pour coffee from the carafe I made earlier. "Here you go." I hand him the drink. I don't add milk or sugar because he likes it black.

It's funny how I've learned small things about Devon like how he likes his coffee or that he's not fond of onions or tomatoes. Or that he doesn't like dancing, but will humor me because I wanted to go.

"Sorry about last night. You were right. That scorpion drink snuck up on me."

"I warned you," he says with a smile, sipping his coffee.

"Yes, you did."

We stare at each other for several beats and then he surprises me by putting down his coffee mug, taking mine out of my hands and placing it on the counter. Then his hand curves around my waist, slides up to my nape. He lowers his mouth to mine. The kiss is slow and sweet and not like our usual passionate coupling.

When he lifts his head, he says, "I missed you last night."

"There's still tonight."

His eyes are aglow with desire and I can't help it—my insides turn to mush.

★ ★ ★

The rest of the day, we don't speak about the end of our relationship. We enjoy the free massages we received from karaoke night and afterward return back to the villa. Devon seems to be comfortable enjoying my company as we sit on the terrace. I'm on the lounger where we've made love countless times while he sways back and forth on the hammock.

The peace I've found here is fleeting. When I go back home, it'll be back to the grind. Being a business owner is completely new to me. I'm used to being a ballerina and being told what to do and how to bend my body to the will of my instructor, choreographer or partner. Those days, however, are long gone.

I'll be teaching new students how to get started in their dance career. They'll be happy and excited and full of hope, like I was. That will have to be enough, since I can no longer dance on the stage.

Admittedly, it won't be easy. I miss performing, and it will take time and patience for me to become a good ballet instructor, but I know I can do it. This week has allowed me to see that I can redefine myself. Ordinarily, I would never have agreed to room with a stranger, let alone been as expressive with my needs, desires and wants as I've been with Devon. This vacation fling has made me see I can take risks not only in my career, but also in my personal life.

If I want to know who my biological mother is, I should arrange a meeting. I can't be afraid, not anymore.

"Are you okay?" Devon asks.

I glance up and find him staring at me. "What?"

"You were frowning. You looked upset."

How would he know if he hadn't been watching me? I offer a smile. We haven't shared our deepest, darkest thoughts or truths, and I'm not about to start now. "I'm fine."

"Are you sure?"

"Yes, absolutely. I'm going to head in and start packing."

What would it be like to have what the other Gems have found, a partner? This week has confirmed for me that I do want to share my life with a special someone. Devon may not want more than a week, but I do. I just wish it were with him, the man who I can talk to, who's awakened my sensuality, who's given me a fresh start.

I don't wait to hear his response and walk back inside the villa. I head into the primary bedroom and pull out my luggage. I'm pulling clothes out of the closet when I see Devon standing in the stairway. His expression is unreadable.

"You don't have to pack now."

"These clothes won't pack themselves."

I swallow the lump forming in my throat and continue taking dresses off the hangers. He stays there, watching me fold clothes and put them in the suitcase, why I don't know. I've accepted that this is ending. I need him to leave so I don't let out the tears threatening in the corners of my eyes. Tears for what will never be. Tomorrow, I'll be leaving not just Aruba, but the joy I've found in being in Devon's arm.

I would love for him to say he wants to continue seeing

me in Memphis, but he doesn't. He's abiding by the rules we set.

So why does it hurt so bad?

"All right then," he replies. "I'll do the same."

I exhale audibly when he's no longer within hearing distance and then I quietly close the door and allow the tears to fall.

Later, after I've put back on my armor, I'm ready to face Devon. He arranged for a sunset champagne cruise so I've put on the dress I was saving for a special night. It's a curve-hugging, one-shoulder black dress with large red roses over the sheer fabric. It flatters and makes me look as if I actually have a figure. I pair it with strappy red sandals and slick my hair back on each side, allowing it to fall in a curtain down my back. I go all out on the makeup, using all the tricks in my arsenal from my ballerina days. The pièce de résistance is a glide of daring red lipstick. I hope to knock Devon's socks off.

When I finally emerge from the bedroom, I find Devon in a sports coat, dress shirt and trousers. He looks devastatingly handsome, and I find I can hardly speak. The O on his lips tells me I've achieved what I wanted.

"Wow!" he exclaims. "You've been holding out on me, Lyric Taylor."

I chuckle. "I couldn't very well show you everything, now could I?"

"Are there any more surprises in store?" he asks with a devilish grin.

"I guess you'll have to wait and see." I sashay past him toward the door, and he rushes over to open it for me.

If this is how it must end, tonight will be on my terms.

Ten

Devon

I knew Lyric was beautiful, but tonight she takes my breath way.

This week was a surprise and a revelation. If ever there was a woman out there who would make me consider dating again, a relationship, possibly introducing them into my daughter's life—it's Lyric.

Since my ex-wife passed, I've been happy with the status quo of brief liaisons. But Lyric—damn her, she has me reconsidering *everything*.

It's like she was made for me, and that's scary as fuck. I'm afraid to go out on a limb with my feelings, even with a woman as amazing as Lyric. Earlier today, I felt her pulling away from me, creating distance between us, and I didn't like it. But what can I do? I'm not offering to change the terms of our deal.

We agreed that what happens in Aruba, stays here.

So I let her hide behind packing her luggage and closing the door. Shutting me out.

It stung.

I wanted to knock and ask her to let me in, and not just through the door, but into her life. I just couldn't bring myself to do it. My marriage did a number on me.

Everything I believed was turned on its head when things didn't work out. I was a romantic and thought everyone had a soulmate and that my ex-wife was mine. She wasn't. I wanted our marriage to be a partnership with two people who loved and respected each other. I believed in forever. I believed love could solve all things.

It didn't.

Sometimes, love isn't enough, especially when one person loves the other more. The way I loved Shiloh more than she loved me. I can't go back to feeling like that. It broke me. I fell into a deep depression after the divorce because I didn't feel good enough, didn't feel *wanted* or *loved*. Kianna was my saving grace and forced me to put one foot in front of the other and keep pushing forward. I couldn't let my child down.

And somehow I've made it through these last few years. I've made it to this trip, this time with Lyric. Maybe that's enough.

Besides, it's not as if Lyric has expressed that she wants to change our arrangement. *And if she did*, an inner voice asks, *would you have agreed?*

I don't think about that. I merely sit beside her on the

way to the marina and remind myself I have one night left. One night to have her again, in every way, in every position imaginable, until dawn breaks and I'm forced to let her go.

Eleven

Lyric

The sunset is a maze of red, orange, pink and purple filling the sky. The champagne is sweet and fizzes just as it should. Yet the night is bittersweet because I know what comes next. I know what tomorrow brings.

I shiver, and Devon removes his sports coat. He doesn't just put it around me, he makes me slide my arms into the garment, which swallows me. I don't mind because the coat smells like him. I inhale his spicy scent in the hopes I'll remember it during the cold nights in my bed alone in Memphis.

I close my eyes, soaking in the moment, and Devon calls me out on it. "Do you always watch the sunset with your eyes closed?"

I open one eye and look at him. "Not usually."

He chuckles and moves behind me so I'm sitting in be-

tween his legs. Then he wraps his arms around me. I wish
we could stay like this forever, but I know it's not possible.
He has a daughter to get back to. LT Dance Academy will
be opening soon, and I can start living my new dream.

After the cruise, we find ourselves at an upscale seafood
restaurant. They sit us outside on the custom-tiled terrace
underneath a pergola with white drapes tied on either end
and a candlelit table for two. With the soft ambient lighting and low instrumental music playing in the background,
the setting is very romantic.

A waiter comes over to introduce himself. He's quite
knowledgeable, and I ask for a starter of oysters on the half
shell.

I didn't eat much earlier because my stomach was in knots
thinking about tomorrow, but oysters have always been my
thing so I savor the dish while perusing the menu. I notice
Devon isn't eating any.

"Don't you like oysters?"

He shakes his head. "Afraid not."

"Why didn't you tell me? We could have ordered something different."

He shakes his head. "I couldn't. I want you to have anything you want tonight."

I don't know what to say to that, so I don't respond and
instead reach for another oyster and stuff my face. Thankfully, the waiter returns with a bottle of very expensive wine
that Devon ordered. I'm not much of a wine aficionado and
only drink the occasional Riesling or moscato, but Devon
makes sure he tastes the selection before accepting it.

When the waiter pours me a glass, Devon inclines his head. "Try it. I promise, you won't be disappointed."

I do and find he's right. It has the perfect amount of crispness without being overly dry.

"Are you ready to order?" the waiter asks, and Devon looks at me.

I order the Aegean Caesar salad and grilled octopus with potatoes and pistachios in a creamy herb sauce, while Devon opts for the honey-glazed salmon with sautéed greens, asparagus and a seafood salad with a sweet honey-soy glaze. Once our orders are complete, the waiter leaves us alone.

"What was your favorite part of the trip?" Devon asks.

I want to say "you," but instead I respond with, "I enjoyed the day we went dancing." It had been too long since I danced just for enjoyment. I was able to be free and become one with the music.

He stares back at me incredulously, and I sense I hurt him with my answer. I try to lighten the mood by asking, "And you? What was your favorite?"

He surprises me with his honesty. "You." He looks at me so intensely I nearly squirm in my seat. I didn't expect him to be so open. My heart stammers in my chest. "Do you care to amend your answer?"

I swallow. "I—I..." My head lowers. If he was able to be honest with me, I can do the same. I glance back up and find his eyes have never left mine. "You know it was you. This week was...*everything.*"

My response causes a broad grin to spread his incredible lips. Lips that I've kissed. Lips that have tasted every part of me. This man has dominated not only my mind, but my body. He awoke a sensuality in me I didn't know existed. With him, I've felt free to discover who I am outside of the ballerina I once was. Agreeing to stay in this villa with him was a risk, normally something I wouldn't have done. This week, however, I'd allowed myself to take all the risks.

"Thank you." He holds up his wineglass. "To us."

I lift mine as well. "To us."

I take a sip, but as I do, his eyes never leave mine. In fact I would say he's focused on my lips, and I know, in that moment, I will be getting very little sleep tonight.

That's all right, I can sleep when I'm in Memphis.

On our way back to the villa after dinner, I lay sprawled across Devon's lap in the taxi. It feels natural to be this close to him. I know it's only for tonight. Tomorrow, we go back to our separate lives.

Part of me believes Devon Masters could very well be *the one*. He's made me feel seen, and not just because of how I look or how compatible we are in the bedroom, but just by being *him*. He's kind, thoughtful and caring, and I've learned that from only a week in his company. Just think how much more I could learn about him, and vice versa, if we had more time...

But I'll never know what we could be to each other. I made an agreement seven days ago without knowing just how good it would be between us.

Yes, the sex is unbelievable, but we have more than that. We can laugh and talk about anything, doesn't matter the topic. So what if he likes *Star Wars* and I like rom-com movies? So what if he's into football and I'd much rather watch gymnastics? We're okay with the other person being different because that's what makes us special.

I'm going to miss *this*, the camaraderie, most of all. I didn't just find a lover in Aruba. I found a friend.

When we arrive back to the villa, we're both quiet, but we don't need words. Instead, I head straight for the bedroom and Devon follows me, watching from the doorway. The feral heat in his gaze is an invitation to pleasure. I see he's already removed his sports coat while I'm trying to remove the strappy sandals, but the latch won't give. Devon comes forward and kneels in front of me. He takes my sandaled foot in his lap and unclasps the latch, first one and then the other, until I'm barefoot.

I move to sit on the bed, but Devon is still on his knees in front of me. He pushes me down until I'm resting on my elbows. I don't understand what's happening until I see him sliding the sheer fabric of my dress over my legs, up to my thighs, until the dress is scrunched at my waist.

"Devon…"

"Shh…" he murmurs, and then I feel him flicking his tongue across my ankle and higher until he reaches the backs of my legs. "You're like a fever in my blood. You're so unguarded and sincere, yet greedy for all the passion and pleasure we've found together. Lyric, I'm burning up with wanting you." He licks a tender spot and then moves upward, pushing my legs apart as he goes. When he reaches my inner thighs, he takes light nips with his teeth and I moan.

How does this man know exactly where to touch me? Yet somehow he does. Because of him, I am comfortable with being vulnerable and allowing someone in. Maybe that was the difference with my other lovers.

I won't forget how being with Devon has helped me love myself and my body again. I know now that I can take risks and come out on the other side stronger than I was before. My life doesn't have to revolve around dance and practicing. I don't have to use my career as a crutch. I can have a rich, fulfilling life, find someone special.

When I feel his hands gliding up my thighs to my thong, I don't fight him. Instead, I let him peel the tiny piece of fabric down my legs and watch him toss it to the floor. He grasps my hips and brings me forward to the edge of the bed. I know what's coming next and I tense.

His eyes are dark with desire when he says, "Relax, I'm going to make you come."

Oh yes, I know, and I can't wait. He dips his head, and I feel his tongue probing between my silken folds. A whimper escapes my lips, especially when he uses his skilled tongue to work his magic. When his lips close around my sensitive clitoris, I sob his name and clutch at his shoulders as my first climax strikes.

But he doesn't stop at one. I can't recover from my first before he's got me climbing toward the second. He slips his hand between my legs and slides a finger deep inside me. Heat floods through me as he stretches me wider, and when he adds another finger and even a third, moving them in an erotic dance, I'm driven higher and higher.

"Devon…" I sob as my second orgasm strikes.

"You want me to stop?" he asks, lifting his head.

"Don't stop, don't stop…please." That's when he uses

both his mouth and fingers to bring me to my third orgasm. I lay on the bed, spent, my legs shaking. When I'm strong enough to finally open my eyes, Devon has already disrobed and put on protection. He's lifting the dress bunched around my waist over my head and unclasping my bra. Then he's nudging my legs apart and easing his solid length inside me. He's being too gentle.

I don't want him gentle. This is our last time together. I want Devon to be wild, to take me with a savage passion, like he did on that very first night. "Harder. Faster," I demand, and reach up to bring his head down to mine.

I claim his lips, kissing him hungrily, sliding my tongue inside his mouth, tasting myself. He groans, but increases the power behind his thrusts. I'm eager, ready for him. I cling to his damp shoulders and move with him, arching my hips to meet him. We're an unstoppable force. A loud cry escapes my lips when my explosive orgasm hits, but Devon doesn't come.

He isn't giving in so easily. Instead, he puts me on all fours and moves behind me. I lower myself onto the bed, lifting my ass into the air so he can take me however he wants. He slides his hand underneath me, teasing me with steady strokes of his fingers.

I'm so turned on that his first thrust feels like heaven. "Yes!"

Devon drives into me deeper and faster. I rake my fingers across the silk sheet desperate for something to grab on to, but there's nothing. I'm his to pleasure.

"That's right, babe," he mutters. "I want it all."

He lifts me up onto my knees and turns my head so his

lips can claim mine again. He sucks on my tongue, while one hand is tweaking my breasts and the other is at my sex, mimicking the actions of his thrusts as he takes me from behind. The sensation of Devon all around me is too much and I climax again, falling forward onto the bed. Only then does Devon pound into me with such fervor, I'm certain I can't take any more pleasure. But when he gives one last powerful thrust, I experience another earth-shattering release as he roars behind me.

Twelve

Lyric

I'm packed. My suitcase is by the door, as is Devon's. I stand at the terrace and look out over the beach one last time. The resort arranged a private car transport for us after the hiccup with the villa, and it'll be here any minute.

Last night was marvelous. I didn't think it was possible to have been made love to so thoroughly. I'm now sporting several hickeys on my neck from where Devon sucked on me on multiple occasions. My breasts feel full and swollen. As for in between my thighs, I'm a bit tender. I lost count of the times Devon made me come.

I didn't let him off the hook easily, either. Over the week, I've learned what he likes, and last night, after he made me come again and again with his mouth and fingers, I got my revenge by taking his dick in my mouth and making him grab me by my hair. He came so hard, he squirted in my mouth, and I licked every drop of him off my lips.

Our lovemaking was more adventurous last night than it had ever been. My flexibility from years of dancing came in handy. I squatted on top of him and took Devon all the way inside and moved him exactly where I wanted him to go. I surprised him further when I spun around and leaned all the way until my back was flat against his chest.

Our movements were slow and sensual as I tightened my pussy around his dick. Devon groaned and fondled my breasts and stroked my clit with his finger. The position had me open and fully exposed, but I felt comfortable with Devon, confident that I could try the maneuver. When his dick hit my G-spot I cried out and nearly lost consciousness.

Devon touches my shoulder and whispers in my ear, bringing me back to the present. "Lyric. The car is here."

I nod and turn around to face him. I start to walk away, but Devon's strong arm closes around me, pulling me back. "One more time." He tangles his fingers in my hair, lowering his head.

He captures my lips in a kiss of pure possession, as if he owns me. And he does. He owns my body. His tongue thrusts deep into my mouth, and I want to melt, but I can't. Slowly, I push against his chest until he releases me. Our breaths are ragged.

"We have to go."

He doesn't say a word, but his eyes tell me he feels regret. For what? For letting me go? He could stop this. He could tell me he wants to be with me in Memphis, but he doesn't.

I've developed feelings for him. I want him to say he wants me. But if he doesn't, that's okay, too. I'm a stronger woman than I was coming to Aruba. Sure, I faced physical difficulties in my career as a ballerina, but I've also learned I can face emotional adversity. I opened myself to Devon more than I have to any other person, even knowing I'd have to leave him behind, and it gives me the strength to know I can do the same when I go home. I will move forward and contact my biological mother, as I've wanted to do for years, because I deserve to know where I come from as I start this new chapter of my life.

I wait several beats and when he says nothing, I walk toward the door and open it.

I don't look behind me as I walk to the car. When the chauffeur sees me, he opens the door and I slide into the back seat. Several minutes tick by as Devon and the driver deal with the luggage. I look resolutely out the window, refusing to watch Devon as he climbs inside the vehicle.

I'm a strong, self-assured Black woman with a full life in Memphis. I have loving parents and amazing friends and sisters in the Gems. LT Dance Academy is opening in a couple of weeks. What more do I need?

Someone to love? my inner voice asks, but I push it down. In this moment, I can't give it credence. If nothing else, my pride prevents me from behaving like some lovesick teenager.

When we arrive at the airport, I put on the emotional mask I need to wear to get through the moment. My face is neutral and devoid of expression. Devon tips the chauffeur and when he reaches for my suitcase, I take it from him, rolling it toward the sliding door.

Our time together is over, and I have to stand on my own two feet. It's time to put on my big-girl pants and tackle the hard stuff.

Because I'm in first class, my boarding area is different from his. I turn to leave, but Devon says, "So, that's it? I don't even get a goodbye?"

My throat is tight, but I spin around to face him. "Goodbye, Devon."

My eyes meet his one last time and I offer a bright smile, then I turn on my heel and walk away. I don't look back. I can't. If I do, I run the risk of throwing myself into his arms and begging him to change our agreement.

I check in and hand my luggage to the attendant at the first-class desk. However, if I go to the gate, Devon will be there. So I head to the VIP lounge that came with my ticket. I stay there as long as possible until they announce our flight will be boarding in ten minutes.

When I finally arrive to the gate, I want to search to see if I can find Devon, but I don't. The break has to be clean. There can't be any backsliding. I move into the line for first-class passengers. The crew begins boarding several minutes later and I rush onto the plane without looking for him. As everyone boards, I keep my head deep in the magazine I'm reading.

That's until I hear a loud cough and glance up to see Devon standing directly in front of me, staring at me while a line forms behind him. His expression is inscrutable. So what if he thinks I gave him the shaft? We agreed that what happens in Aruba, stays here. He could have asked me to change things, but he didn't.

"Sir." A flight attendant comes to stand in front of Devon. "Do you need assistance? If not, can you keep the line moving?"

Devon blinks several times as if he's bringing her into focus. "No, I don't need anything. I don't need anyone." And he brushes past me.

My heart sinks at his words. *I don't need anyone.*

He needed me on the island. Wanted me. I felt as if I was his next breath, but apparently, I was just a warm body ready and willing to do anything.

"Madam," the flight attendant comes to my row. "Would you like some champagne?"

"Yes, keep them coming."

It's the only way I'm going to get through this flight knowing Devon is behind me.

My priority bags come out quickly when we arrive at Memphis International Airport and I head curbside to wait for my father. As soon as we landed, I texted him and he responded he was in the waiting lot and would be here in ten minutes. Since it's January and cold out, I opened my luggage inside the terminal and pulled out the winter jacket I had with me before I embarked on this journey.

Was I really in a tropical climate hours ago? Now it all seems like a dream.

True to his word. My dad arrives within ten minutes in his Lincoln Nautilus. My dad isn't flashy and prefers reliability over fanciness. When he sees me, he hops out of the SUV and pulls me into a bear hug. "Lyric!"

It's so good to see him. "I missed you, Daddy." I return his embrace.

I notice several people stare at us awkwardly. A large Caucasian man with a beard wearing a polo and jeans is hugging me, a Black woman, and kissing my forehead. I turn my head and see Devon walking out of the terminal at that exact moment.

His eyes meet mine, and I see precisely when he thinks that I've somehow betrayed him with another man. Devon looks at me as if I'm a cheater and have been messing around with him while I had someone else at home. His gaze is icy as he storms down the sidewalk.

Who cares what he thinks?

It's not my problem he's jumping to the wrong conclusion.

"You ready to go, pumpkin?"

I nod and my dad grabs my suitcase from me, putting it in the trunk.

He opens my door and I slide into the passenger seat. Then he comes around to the driver's side.

As we pull away from the curb, I can't help but notice Devon's eyes are burning bright and hot. He's staring after our car and his hurt is evident. Then, just as quickly, the flame dies and his gaze is nothing but cold. A well of disappointment and pain opens up inside me. I never told him my parents were Caucasian, but I shouldn't have had to tell him. If I said I wasn't seeing anyone, he should believe me, but it's clear he doesn't. He thinks I lied to him.

And that hurts.

But our weeklong Aruba fling is over. It's back to the real world.

A world without Devon.

Thirteen

Devon

I knew I couldn't trust her.

She has another man at home while she is gallivanting in Aruba with me? How is it possible that the sincere woman of this past week could have lied to me?

Knowing that I was wrong about her stings.

Being with Lyric gave me hope for the future, made me realize I shouldn't paint every woman with the same brush. Not everyone is my ex-wife. Lyric made me believe I could find love again if I was willing to be vulnerable, to trust. But just like that, my hope for the future is ripped to shreds. Seeing Lyric hug another man so soon after what we shared…

I think I'm mostly angry with myself for actually hoping for a second chance at love. I was starting to let go of the past, to embrace the present and finally trust someone.

Until Lyric, it's been difficult letting anyone in. But because of our time together, I was looking toward a future where I might find happiness, and now this.

I should have known something was up when she was cold and unfeeling at the villa and the airport. I hoped that, like me, she was having a hard time accepting the end of our relationship.

Instead, I find she has a man waiting for her. And not any man, some Caucasian guy who is old enough to be her father. Is she his mistress? His side piece? How can she let herself be used this way?

I don't know why I care, but I do. She pulled away from me the second we left the villa and what did I do? I let her. I was afraid to speak up because what could I say when I wasn't offering to see her again in Memphis? Instead, I sat silently beside her the entire ride to the airport. I wanted to reach out and pull her into my lap, demand she give us a chance. But I didn't, even though I could feel the tension emanating from her side of the car. She stared out the window as if there was something more fascinating than the two of us going on out there.

And at the airport, she barely hazarded me a goodbye before she sashayed her fine ass to first class only to ignore me on the plane. I suspect she pulled away from me because of the tight connection we found in Aruba. I feel the same. We shared an incredible week, one I won't soon forget. Couldn't she tell how hard it was for me to walk away without knowing when I might see her again? I'm saddened that the woman I thought I knew doesn't exist.

All I can do is focus on the here and now. I'm coming

back home to my daughter—who right now is waving furiously as Chantel brings her Nissan Rogue to the curb. The car door flies open and Kianna flings herself into my open arms. I scoop her up, catching her as I always will.

There's nothing and no one I love in the world more than her.

"Daddy, I missed you!" Kianna says, wrapping her small arms around my neck. I rise to my feet, pulling my suitcase along to the car.

"I missed you, too, baby girl." I give her a kiss on the cheek.

Chantel is opening the trunk. "Welcome back, Devo." My sister calls me by the nickname she gave me years ago. "How was the trip?"

"Nice, but uneventful." I take the suitcase and with one hand place it in the trunk.

A total lie.

I fell for a slender beauty with the body of a goddess. We made love in every way imaginable until my eyes were crossed only to then find out she has a sugar daddy on the side. Oh no, I'm not telling this story to anyone. I'll take it to my grave. I already made a fool out of myself once for love. I don't intend to do it again.

"I'm glad. You needed to get away and reset." She presses a kiss to my cheek since Kianna seems intent on not letting me go.

I slide into the back seat with Kianna where she regales me with stories about her entire week and what she did in first grade. It's good to be back, but if I'm honest I'm going to miss a pair of beautiful almond-shaped brown eyes looking at me as she sobs out my name when I'm buried deep inside her.

Damn you, Lyric.

We stay at Chantel's for dinner because it's easier than me trying to scrounge something up when I've been gone for a week. Besides, Kianna enjoys spending time with her cousins, my sister's children, my nephew Amir and niece Aniya.

Once we're back home in our three-bedroom, two-and-a-half bath in Germantown a couple hours later, I get Kianna ready for bed. While I was out frolicking on an island, Chantel was taking Kianna back and forth to school each day.

Now it's time to get Kianna back to our routine. After she's brushed her teeth and put on her pj's, I join her in her pink-and-white bedroom that's decorated with everything unicorn. She has an obsession with them, and I gave in and ordered a new bedspread with a rainbow unicorn on it a few months back.

I tuck her in and ask, "What story would you like tonight, sweetheart?" She likes when I read to her before bed.

"*More than a Princess*." She loves the book because the princess's name is Kiana, similar to hers.

When Shiloh died, Kianna had terrible nightmares, fearing I might leave, too. Although they didn't have a strong relationship and I had primary custody, Kianna still knows she lost her mother. I don't know if she fully understands what that means, but I tried my best to explain her mommy is in heaven with the angels.

I was happy to have Kianna living with me because she

provided me comfort after my disastrous marriage. Caring for Kianna made me feel wanted and loved. So, for a while, during the nightmares, she slept with me. When she started kindergarten, however, she told me she was a big girl and wanted to sleep in her own bed. She wanted her independence and had learned I would always be there for her. But I have to say, I miss cuddling her in my arms. She was a safety net for me, too. Now she sleeps alone in her room, which is right next to mine.

As I read to her, I notice her eyes slowly start to close. Kianna tries to fight it, but the lull of my voice soon makes her drift off to sleep. When I'm sure she's under, I tuck in the covers nice and tight, lay the book on her nightstand to finish up tomorrow and turn off the lights.

Today has been a day.

This morning, I woke up with Lyric in my arms, her warm, naked body nestled against mine after our marathon lovemaking session that lasted well into the night and morning. We'd passed out around 4:00 a.m., so I got very little sleep.

Was it really just this morning we were together? Somehow, it seems longer, especially after finding out she was using me while she had another man, an older man, waiting for her at home. Is that what's bothering me, the fact that he's older? White? Or is it that there was another man at all?

Definitely the latter.

I wanted to be the only man.

I know that's foolish when day one I made the rules and stated we would have a short-lived affair on the island. The way she looked at me spoke to something deep in my soul.

Without my realizing, I let her in and began to trust her. For a little while, she showed me it was okay to be vulnerable.

Not anymore. It was hard enough to trust anyone after Shiloh passed. Women I met wanted to offer me comfort, but weren't necessarily interested in becoming a stepmother. I discovered that pretty quickly when they acted as if Kianna didn't exist when they came over with a casserole.

I'm protective of my baby girl. Because Kianna was young, I felt it necessary to keep other women at arm's length. Shiloh hurt us both. She made promises she didn't keep, which left me feeling unwanted and left Kianna without a mother. So I built armor around myself to keep from getting hurt again.

But Lyric?

She got to me. She broke through the barriers I thought I had fortified. Lyric made me reconsider the no dating or relationships vow I adopted after my divorce. She made me want to trust again. I feel like a fool for having believed her. She shared herself with me when she had another man waiting in Memphis. She broke my trust in her.

I will refortify the barriers around my heart and ensure no one will break through them ever again.

Fourteen

Lyric

"I want to hear all about your trip," my father says when instead of heading to my town house as I hoped so I can unpack, he takes me to my parents'. "Your mom made dinner." He reads my mind. "She thought you wouldn't want to have to figure out a meal."

"You guys are the best."

"And the trip?" he asks as we drive down the highway.

"Incredible. The villa the Gems got for me was amaze balls. It was right on the beach with a hammock, pool and hot tub."

"That sounds great. Did you meet anyone new on the trip?"

My mind wanders to Devon and the smiles he would give me when he thought I wasn't looking. But then I remember the scornful look he sent in my direction when we left the airport. He thinks I'm seeing my dad. He thinks I was dishonest when I said there was no one else but him. He clearly has trust issues. And it's not as if I can correct him because I'll never see him again.

He got his wish. What happens in Aruba, stays there.

"No one special," I respond to my father's question. "It was just nice to get away before the grand opening of LT Dance Academy."

He hazards me a quick glance. "Have I told you how proud your mother and I are of you?"

"Ummm... I don't recall." I laugh.

He chuckles. "Well, we are. You've worked so hard. We're so proud to see you moving past your injury to a new dream."

My parents invested a lot of time and money into ensuring I received the very best ballet instruction. Often, my father worked overtime to ensure I had a few extra hours at the studio. He even left Memphis for a while to take another job in San Antonio, before eventually deciding to come back to his hometown. And when my ballet outfits became too expensive, my mom took up sewing and learned how to make tutus herself. She became so good, she had her own side business for other ballerinas, but she always made sure mine looked the best.

"I know, Daddy. Thank you. But it still feels like I let you down." It was my greatest regret that I couldn't give them back half of what they'd sacrificed for me.

He reaches across the console and touches my arm. "Lyric, we have never blamed you. You shouldn't feel guilty. It's not your fault."

A tear trickles down my cheek. I know that in my head, but not in my heart.

"We love you, Lyric. Our love isn't conditional. We love you whether you're a ballerina with a major dance company or a business owner."

I inhale deeply and nod. I stare out the window. My dad understands. He allows me to take a few minutes to collect myself. Sometimes, the pain catches me at unexpected moments. I have tried to make my peace with not dancing professionally and becoming a teacher. I'm hoping the studio will allow my love of ballet to return and give me some comfort at seeing my students go on to do great things.

We pull into my parents' ranch-style home in Collierville, a middle-class town with tree-lined streets, where everyone knows one another. I grew up on this street and was the only Black kid in my neighborhood. It was difficult learning how to assimilate when I didn't look like any of the kids in my class.

Children aren't always kind. I was called names and picked on because my hair wasn't straight enough or my skin was too dark and because I didn't have the pale complexion of other girls my age. During the summer, I stayed out of the sun, refusing to go to the beach for fear of getting too dark because ballerinas were always supposed to be pale and ethereal. Eventually, kids at school got used to me as the Taylors' Black kid and left me alone.

The feelings of insecurity, like I didn't belong, didn't go away as I got older. I never fit in at school or as a ballerina. I was seen as less than by my peers and quickly learned to shut off my emotions. Never let 'em see you sweat. I refused to give anyone the power to let them know they hurt me. It allowed me to endure the body-shaming and name-calling. However, in closing myself off from the hurt caused by their taunts, I also closed myself off from feeling anything real and true.

Until Devon.

"Here we are." Daddy shuts off the engine. I hop out and follow him inside my family home.

My parents recently renovated the four-bedroom, two-bath house. They added new hardwood floors and a gourmet kitchen and refaced the former brick fireplace so it's all black and white now.

Mama greets me in the living room. She's five-foot-three with mousy brown hair, a heart-shaped face and big brown eyes. Mama is diminutive in stature with pearly white skin and a wide smile. I remember growing up and wishing I had skin like hers.

"Lyric." She rushes toward me and pulls into me a hug. "Welcome home."

"Thanks, Mama. It's good to be back." To something familiar and not the crazy sensual roller coaster I've been on the last week.

"Are you hungry?" she asks once she releases me. "I made your favorite. Spinach lasagna."

My stomach chooses that moment to growl. I couldn't eat much on the plane and picked at my food. How could I eat when Devon was in the rear of the plane? I didn't know if he would try to talk to me.

"Yes, I would love some." Dad and I follow her into the kitchen and I take a seat at the eat-in kitchen table for four while she moves around making me a plate. Dad grabs a beer from the fridge and joins me at the table.

"Tell us about the trip," Mama says with her back turned. "What did you do?"

My traitorous mind goes to Devon and all the fun moments we had, from frolicking on the beach to strolling down the promenade to karaoke to game night. "Mostly, I laid out on the beach at the resort," I respond. "I did some swimming and snorkeling, went into town, did a little shopping and took a city tour to learn about the history of Aruba."

"Sounds fantastic. It was so nice of the girls to give you this gift. I can't believe that nearly fifteen years later, you're still friends."

I shrug. "What can I say, Mama? Everyone made a conscious decision to put in the effort. Though it's a little harder these days with everyone coupling up."

"How do you feel about that?" Daddy chimes in to the conversation.

Mama comes over with my plate of lasagna as well as one for Daddy. Once she's made hers and we say grace, I dive right into the meal.

"I admit it's not easy seeing Wynter, Egypt, Asia and now Shay find their happily-ever-after. I want that, too, but I have to believe my time will come."

"It will, honey," Mama says, patting my hand. "I kissed a lot of frogs before your father came along." She gives my father a conspiratorial wink.

Her words resonate, and I determine in that moment

not to think about the past but to focus on my future and what's coming next.

LT Dance Academy is opening in two short weeks. There's a lot to be done, but I feel relaxed and ready for the task at hand. Although I'm saddened that the week with Devon ended on a sour note, at the end of the day, the experience gave me a new lease on life. I got in touch with a brand-new me. A woman who is self-assured and confident in her sexuality, a woman not afraid to take risks.

Being a business owner and teacher is a new identity for me, but I feel like I'm capable of doing anything I put my mind to, including reaching out to my birth mother and finally learning about my past.

My father eventually drops me off at my town house later that evening. It feels strange being alone after having nonstop company for twenty-four hours a day for the last week. I'm usually sad after a Six Gems trip when I have to come home to an empty house. Tonight feels that way. I miss the companionship I had with Devon even though I know it was all temporary.

A moment in time.

Without my parents' twenty-questioning me, I can finally let my emotions run free. I bottled them up because that was the only way I could get through the day. I'm upset Devon didn't try to fight for us. Could I have fought for us? I suppose I could have spoken up. Told him how much our week together meant to me, but I was afraid of rejection.

Rejection has always been a particularly sticky subject for me.

I guess it boils down to being adopted and finding out my birth mother didn't want me. Logically, I know she was sixteen and too young to be a mother, but the other part of me, the part that wants to belong, hates that she didn't even try. I know I have a lot to be thankful for. I was adopted by wonderful parents who love me as their own and gave me anything and everything my heart desired. Yet something has always been missing. I want to know where I belong. I want to know who my real family is.

I wonder what my biological mother, Athena, is like. Do we resemble each other? Do I have her almond-shaped eyes, her nose or mouth? Are there similar character traits? What's her body type? Is she slender and willowy or do I take after my father?

Speaking of which—who is he? The attorney didn't have any info because Athena left his name off the birth certificate, but I would like to know. I'm not sure if I'll search for him or not, but a name would be a start.

So much is whirling through my mind—Devon, Athena, LT Dance Academy—that I leave my luggage downstairs and climb the steps to my bedroom. I strip and take a hot shower, hoping to clear my head and find some peace. I step inside the walk-in shower and let the water sluice down my body. I grasp my sponge, add soap and smooth it over my shoulders, breasts, stomach and thighs.

I daydream of Devon as he lathered my body. I close my eyes and allow my mind to go back there, to the moment when he discarded the sponge and used his fingers to slip between my legs. It's a poor substitute to have my own fingers move down my damp folds and slide inside. Heat

floods my veins and I envision Devon using his fingers to
move inside me.

It feels so good, I move my fingers a bit faster, desperate
to find release. I pump my fingers in and out of my pussy
until eventually a sob escapes and I fall backward against the
cold tiles. My eyes pop open and I remember where I am.

At home.

Alone.

I tell myself not to cry and blink back tears, but it's no
use. I allow them to fall down my cheeks along with the
water from the shower. I miss Devon. He opened me up
sexually and sensually to the woman lying underneath all
the insecurities. A beautiful, sexy, confident Black woman.
But he's gone and never coming back and I need to figure
out what I want.

And I will. On my own terms.

Fifteen

Lyric

I look around one of the studios in my three-thousand-square-foot facility in amazement. My new dream has become a reality.

Another dance studio located here recently closed, so I was able to purchase the building and renovate the space to suit my needs. I have four studios with high ceilings, new lighting, vinyl flooring that looks like hardwood, expansive mirrors, permanent and mobile ballet barres and a state-of-the-art music system with BOSE speakers as well as large viewing windows with blinds if I need to block out too-attentive parents.

But I didn't do this alone or in a vacuum.

Wynter's aunt, Helaine Smith, gifted me and the other Gems with a small inheritance. I was as surprised as the other Gems when the lawyer read the will. I am forever thankful for Helaine's kindness because when I lost ballet, I was devastated and unsure of what to do next with my life. The injury I sustained to my leg was life-changing, cutting short my dance career.

Ballet had been my entire world, so much so that after the accident I vowed to never dance again. But then, the Gems came to visit me in San Francisco, where I'd been working at the San Francisco Ballet. I had been holed up in my tiny apartment for weeks, in a deep depression and unable to move. My parents had tried unsuccessfully to pull me out of that state, so they called in reinforcements.

Teagan and Shay physically lifted me out of bed and put me in a bath while the rest of the Gems cleaned up the apartment and opened up the windows, allowing fresh air in. They bathed and dressed me, refusing to let me wallow in grief and despair.

Even when I didn't talk, they fluttered around me chatting about their lives until eventually I broke down, crying and crying. They held me in their arms and told me I would get through it. Wynter offered to pay for therapy to ensure I had someone to talk to once my friends were gone.

But it was Teagan who suggested the dance studio.

"I know you can't dance professionally, but you're an amazing dancer, Lyric. Maybe you could teach? Help others find their dreams."

I shook my head, unable to even consider it, but slowly—after leaving San Francisco with my hopes and dreams in tatters and returning to Memphis with my parents—Teagan's idea began to take shape. Perhaps I could give my passion a new outlet? My dance instructors had once been dancers themselves, and they'd made a career of teaching. I called Aleksandr Smirnov and we spent a wonderful day together, laughing and talking about the past.

Aleksandr helped me see it wasn't just a possibility, but could be a reality. I didn't know how I was going to do it. I didn't have any money because I'd never done anything except dance. My parents suggested I get a loan, and I was in the middle of the process when Helaine's gift came.

It was a miracle.

And now, today, it's the grand opening of LT Dance Academy. I'm having the event catered. Thanks to some help from my parents and one of their friends, an event planner, the studio has been elegantly decorated. There are high-top tables sprinkled sporadically on the back side of the larger studio space, which will eventually be perfect for recitals and other intimate performances. In the corner a huge balloon backdrop is set up so attendees can take photos and post them on social media.

Word of mouth is going to be huge. It's what makes or breaks most studios.

"The place looks amazing," Mama says, coming toward me with her arms outstretched.

I squeeze her hands. "Thank you. I hope today is a success." I had a press release sent to several local media outlets and hope to receive some positive coverage.

"Don't worry."

"I agree with your mama," Daddy replies, coming into the room. He's been moving boxes and helping me set up my office over the last couple of days. I have a brand new

Ikea desk, chair and file cabinets. It looks like a bona fide office to conduct business.

I'm a business owner.

"Can anyone else get in on this action?" A chorus of feminine voices asks from the doorway.

I glance up to see Wynter and Shay standing inside the studio. My parents step aside and make way for them.

"It's so good to see you guys." I rush toward the women and they squeeze me in a hug.

"I've missed you, darling," Shay replies once we've all parted.

I've always admired Shay's sleek athletic figure. I'm willowy thanks to ballet, but Shay is killing it in a denim zipper dress that shows baby got back! Her toffee skin gleams and her dark brown locs are in an elaborate twist I know she didn't do. Had to have been Wynter.

Speaking of Wynter—marriage suits her. She's never looked lovelier. Her usual dark waves have grown out and now reach below her shoulders, but she hasn't lost her killer curves, shown off in a rib-knit dress. "This place looks great, Lyric. I know Auntie Helaine would be so proud of you for making your dreams come true."

"I couldn't have done it without her."

It's been a lot of hard work, but the ladies were a great resource. Egypt has her restaurant, Flame, while Asia's jewelry store, Six Gems, and Shay's yoga studio, Balance and Elevate, are thriving. It's the queen bee Teagan, though, who takes the cake. Her brokerage business was under way long before Helaine's gift gave her an added boost.

"I do believe this trio is missing half of us," Egypt says,

holding up three fingers as she sashays through the door. Tall and bold, Egypt's got buckets of confidence, but I suppose the love of a good man can do that. Egypt's long ebony tresses are in a side ponytail, and she's dressed in a chartreuse midi dress that shows off her bountiful breasts.

"Divas in the house!" Teagan yells, and comes in behind Egypt with petite Asia bringing up the rear, pushing a baby stroller. If she's not in a signature suit, Teagan is in a sheath dress with her staple sleek short haircut. This sheath dress is emerald, but if anyone can pull it off it's Teagan.

What's most intriguing is that one of us is now a mom.

Asia had Ryan months ago, and we were all present to witness the sacred event. I walk over to her and the little tyke. I peer inside the stroller to see the cutest baby with skin of the color of wheat and the chubbiest cheeks that I have to squeeze. He's wearing a plaid shirt, tan pants and adorable baby Jordan sneakers.

"O-M-G, Asia, he's an absolute doll," I gush.

"And what am I, chicken liver?" Asia pouts with her hands on her hips. I forget Asia is used to being the center of attention in our group, but now that she's had Ryan, we all fuss over him.

"You know I love you, girl." I lean over and squeeze her shoulders. "And I must say, does baby weight even exist, because it doesn't look as if you have any?"

Asia beams at my words and smooths down the leather pants she's wearing with an off-the-shoulder cheetah-print sweater. "Oh, what can I say, I've been hitting the gym hard. This little guy," she glances down into the stroller, "made me gain thirty-five pounds. I lost twenty as soon as I had him, but thanks to breastfeeding the other fifteen came off easily."

"Jesus, is this what we're reduced to?" Teagan asks. "Talking about babies and breastfeeding?" She sighs dramatically. "I thought we were here to celebrate LT Dance Academy."

"That's right!" Egypt responds with a snap. "We need to turn up. Where's the music?"

And that's how the grand opening celebration for LT Dance Academy kicks off. The Six Gems' arrival brings the rest of the attendees. Most are parents and some are soon-to-be students. Aleksandr attends as well and raves about the studio. The turnout is great, and I couldn't be prouder. I never thought I'd be in this position. I thought I would be a ballerina with a major company for many more years, but if I can't have that, the academy is the next best thing.

I give a few tours of the facilities, showing parents and students the different types of studios available and talking about the variety of class offerings. There are a few Caucasian women who walk in with their daughters. I see they're surprised that, I, a Black woman, am the owner. I try not to let their pessimism get to me.

"Ignore them," Shay says, coming to my side when she notices a few of them whispering. "I've had to deal with the same kind of people. They assume Black people don't enjoy yoga, let alone own a studio. Don't let them steal your joy."

"I won't." I'm used to their type. Racism and colorism are rampant in the ballet industry. Most folks are not used to people of color dancing ballet, but that's okay because I've always been up for the challenge.

Before the crowd starts to dissipate, I ask everyone to grab a cup of their favorite beverage—for the kids, it's punch, for adults, it's a glass of champagne.

"I want to thank you all for coming today. LT Dance Academy is a labor of love. Ballet has been in my blood since I was five years old. I want to thank my parents—" I motion Mama and Daddy over to join me and hear the shocked gasps among the crowd "—for introducing me to something I love and for supporting me over the last two and a half decades. Because of you—" tears choke my voice, but I beat them back "—I was able to dance professionally with the San Francisco Ballet before an injury changed my future, but my journey isn't over. My love of ballet, and many more genres, will continue here as I help the next generation of dancers learn to love dance as much I do. Cheers." I hold up my champagne flute.

Everyone in the crowd joins me in the toast and takes a sip of their respective beverages.

A few hours later, however, the event is dying down and I find I'm exhausted. The days leading up to the grand opening and all the hype have worn me out.

"What a great day," Mama says. "Your father and I are so very proud of you. You did good, Lyric."

Large grins are on both their faces as they hug me once more. "Go ahead and spend time with the Gems," my father replies. "We'll be here to celebrate long after they're gone."

"Thanks, Daddy." I kiss his cheek.

Just then a beautiful little girl with two big pigtails and smooth peanut-butter skin comes my way. I bend down until I can look at her. "And what's your name?"

"I'm Kianna."

"Hi, Kianna. I'm Ms. Taylor. Are you interested in dance?"

She nods her head and then looks back at a tall woman with lovely braids down her back. "Yes, she is. My name is Chantel Dixon, and I've enrolled her in your program for four- to six-year-olds."

"Excellent. Is there a form of dance you prefer?" I ask Kianna.

"I want to be like you. I want to be a ballerina." Kianna responds and to my amazement, attempts a pirouette.

And she's good.

I clap my hands. "Nice! Ballet is hard work, Kianna, but if you really want it, anything is possible." I turn to the woman I assume is her mother. "If you need any help with getting her prepared for class, please let me know."

"Thank you. We'll see you on Saturday." The first day of classes at LT Dance Academy.

I nod my head and watch them walk away. At the door, however, Kianna turns and gives me a little wave.

"I see the makings of another Lyric with that one," Shay says from my side.

I think so. I'm encouraged to see a student so young have so much joy and passion. I remember myself at that age, before all the classes, private training and recitals. At the time, I couldn't wait to learn. I soaked up everything like a sponge. Maybe I can find my love of ballet again in children like Kianna.

I desperately want to. I wasn't lying when I said I wanted to help the next generation. I lost my love of the art after I couldn't dance professionally. It was a hard adjustment after so many years of devoting myself to the genre. In Aruba, I learned that I could dance again just for fun and *feel* the music flow through me.

Maybe one day, I can find my joy in ballet again.

Sixteen

Devon

I'm so late picking up Kianna, but it couldn't be avoided.

The last few weeks have been a bear, getting caught up after coming back from vacation. Not only that, a new project was dropped in my lap at work, which kept me at the office longer than I intended. I'm racing now through traffic to get to my sister's. A stay-at-home mom, Chantel does a lot for me and is my backup in case work gets in the way, which it sometimes does.

If I can, I try to pick up Kianna up from school. We'll go out for ice cream or a yogurt. Sometimes, we'll go to the park and I'll push her on the swing or let her run around and burn off some energy. I may only be thirty-two, but my God, Kianna has loads of energy. And after a long day at the office, I sometimes have to force myself to get into Daddy mode.

She deserves the very best of me, no matter how tired I am. I'm the only parent she has. I have to be both Daddy and Mommy, and it can be a tad exhausting. Once, my sister schooled me about being more caring and empathetic if Kianna fell and had a boo-boo. I had to learn how to kiss it and make it better and give her a princess Band-Aid.

I feel guilty when I don't show up on time to a school event or am late because of work. It's why, after Shiloh's death, I changed my hours to end at four thirty. My boss is understanding because I usually forgo lunch. But today, it's nearly 6:00 p.m. when I pull into Chantel's driveway and turn off the engine.

As I approach her mid-century modern home, I hear music. I use the key Chantel gave me and walk into the living room in time to see Kianna all dolled up like a ballerina, along with my niece, while my sister watches from the couch. Both girls are wearing leotards, rainbow tutus, pink tights and ballet shoes.

Kianna is whirling around the room and executing movements I haven't seen since...well, since her mother.

As if it were yesterday, I can envision Shiloh prancing around the dance studio after she forgot a dinner with me or failed to pick up Kianna for the weekend. All I can think about is how her dance career came first, before our marriage, before our little girl. I see red.

"What the hell is going on?" I yell over the music.

Startled, Kianna immediately stops dancing and Chantel jumps up from the sofa. "Devon, I—I didn't hear you come in." She quickly reaches for the remote and turns off the music.

I notice both the girls look like they're ready to cry because I'm unable to hide the fury on my face. It's coursing through my veins. How dare she? Chantel knows how I feel about dancing. Hell, it had taken Lyric to get me out on the dance floor because I hadn't danced in years. The only reason I'd gone out when we were in Aruba was because other men were watching Lyric and I hadn't wanted them to touch her. I wanted them to know she was *mine*.

"I'm sorry, Daddy," Kianna responds, tears streaming down her cheeks.

I inhale deeply and tell myself to calm down. I don't like seeing Kianna upset. "It's okay, sweetheart. Chantel, can I speak to you outside?" I ask curtly.

Chantel nods, and I don't bother waiting to see if she follows me out the front door. Once we're outside, I let my sister have it. "What the hell, Chantel?"

She motions her hand lower. "Calm down, Devon. They were just dancing." I glare at her, but surprisingly my sister doesn't back down and stares right back at me. "It's not a crime."

"No. But you know how I feel about the subject," I respond hotly, pacing back and forth on the porch.

"Yes, I do, and it's completely irrational. A lot of kids go to dance class, Devon. It's a popular activity."

"How dare you judge me? You have no idea what I went through during my marriage and divorce."

"No, I don't, because you refuse to talk about it. You're closed up as tight as a tortoise. Just because you have an issue with dancing doesn't make it Kianna's issue. I'm sorry I went against your wishes, but I'm her aunt. And I promised myself when Shiloh died that I would be there for my niece. Be the woman in her life when she needs someone to talk to."

"And I appreciate that, I do." I rub my hand across my head. "You've been a great help to me, and I know you love Kianna, but you know how I feel about dancing." I try to be the voice of reason when I feel far from it. I don't want dance to have any place in my house. I thought I exorcised it when Shiloh left us.

"Of course I do, Devon, *but she came to me. What was I supposed to do?*"

Her response hits me in the chest, knocking me off-kilter, and I stop pacing.

"She did?"

"She told me she wants to dance like her mother and thought I could help. Apparently, she saw some videos when she was at her grandparents' house."

I allow Shiloh's parents, Kianna's grandparents, to take Kianna for weekends sometimes. They miss their daughter, and having Kianna around brings them so much joy. I don't begrudge them that, but also don't want them filling Kianna's head with visions of being a dancer like her mother. They know how I feel on the subject, too, but apparently another talk is in order.

"I see. Well, that explains it, but you should have spoken to me first before buying her all that stuff. How much do I owe you? I'll return it all."

"You can't!" Chantel hisses. "It will break Kianna's heart. She's so excited. She enjoyed her first ballet class. She was so looking forward to showing you everything she learned. It's why she was still in her costume."

"Damn it, Chantel!" I lower my head and rub my neck. I can feel tension forming there and the beginnings of a headache. If I pull the rug from underneath Kianna's feet, she'll be upset with me. I don't want that. I don't like seeing my baby girl crying but I also don't like the fact that she's dancing. It reminds me too much of Shiloh. Dancing always came first.

"Daddy?" I hear Kianna's small voice from the front door and turn around to face her. I hate the despair I see in her eyes. I don't know how much she's heard, but she knows I can snatch ballet from her. "Do I have to give up ballet class? I don't want to, it's so much fun."

I turn and glare at Chantel. How can I deny my daughter something she wants so badly? At least not right now. However, I could just wait and see how this pans out. This could be a fad. Children have passing interests all the time. She could get bored with this very easily and move on to another sport, but if I say it's forbidden, it will make her want it all the more. So I give in. I don't want Kianna lying or keeping things from me. I want us to be open and honest with each other. Besides, she's too young to understand the complicated relationship I had with her mother.

I put on the best fake smile I can and say, "Of course you don't. I didn't know because your auntie didn't tell me. It's why Daddy was so upset."

"So I can still go?" Kianna asks, hopefully.

I nod.

"Thank you, Daddy." She rushes to me and wraps her

small arms around my waist. I swing her up and into my arms and give my sister an angry glare as we go inside. This is far from over, but I'll table it for now.

We don't stay for dinner at Chantel's. I advise her to send me all the information on the dance school so I can check it out for myself. I assume my sister did her due diligence and researched the teacher to make sure it was safe to take Kianna and Aniya, but I'll feel better after I look into it. That's when Chantel informs me the next class is the day after tomorrow.

Great, just how I was looking to spend my weekend. However, I have no choice but to assume a happy disposition because Kianna decides to share her excitement about the topic and how Ms. Taylor is so nice and explains everything so well.

The last name gives me pause and butterflies swarm my stomach. Visions of almond-shaped eyes and a willowy frame wearing an itty-bitty bikini while lounging on an Aruban terrace comes to mind.

Taylor.

Lyric's last name is Taylor, but they couldn't possibly be one and the same, could they? Memphis is a big place and Taylor is a common name. I dismiss the idea, but as I lay my head on my pillow after finishing reading the princess book to Kianna, I dream of her.

Her auburn hair.

Her soft café au lait skin against mine.

And the way she screamed my name when I was buried to the hilt inside her.

Why can't I get her out of my mind?

★ ★ ★

To stop myself from thinking about Lyric, I decide to confront the culprits who started us down this path. Shiloh's parents. Charmaine and Nick Baldwin are good people, but they should have minded their own business and not shown Kianna those videos.

When I call, Charmaine picks up on the third ring, "Devon, how wonderful to hear from you. How was your trip?"

"It was great, thank you." My response is clipped and curt.

"Is everything okay? You sound upset."

"No, I'm not okay," I respond hotly. "In fact, I'm rather upset and would like to talk to you and Nick. Can you put him on the phone?"

"Yes, yes, of course." I hear her shuffling and a few moments later, I hear Nick's voice.

"Devon, what's wrong? Charmaine told me you're upset with us? Why?"

"Did you show Kianna videos of Shiloh dancing?"

There's silence on their end, and then Charmaine speaks. "We didn't see the harm, Devon. Kianna is our granddaughter, and we just want her to know her mother."

I sigh and some of my anger dissipates. "I get that, I do, but you should have discussed it with me first."

"Is that really necessary?" Nick responds, and I can tell he's agitated. "It was just a video."

"I want Kianna's focus to be on academics."

"Meaning you want all parts of Shiloh wiped away?"

Nick counters. "Kianna deserves to know who her mother was. Dance was a huge part of Shiloh's life."

"That may be so, but at the end of the day, Kianna is *my* daughter and I decide what's right or wrong for her. Do we understand each other?"

I hear Nick huffing and puffing in the background, but in the end Charmaine responds. "We understand, but we need you to be a bit more compassionate. We lost our daughter, and the videos keep her alive in our hearts. We were just sharing that with Kianna."

And now I feel like an asshole. Nick is right. I shouldn't be coming down on them. They love their daughter and were just sharing part of that love with Kianna. "You're right. I'm sorry. I guess I'm just touchy when it comes to dancing. It played a big role in the disintegration of my marriage."

"We know. We're thankful you've allowed us to be a part of Kianna's life," Charmaine adds.

"You don't have to thank me. You're Kianna's family and you always will be. I'm sorry for having called. You both have a good night." I hang up as quickly as I can. I feel like a fool for overreacting, but my emotions are all over the place.

I know why.

I feel like my trust is being tested from all sides. Kianna going to Chantel about wanting to dance. Chantel not telling me about Kianna wanting to attend ballet class, and the Baldwins sharing a dance video. It all started with losing trust and faith in Lyric. After the week we shared, I had high hopes of moving on with my life and embracing dating and relationships again. I thought I was ready to trust again, but she lied to me, too, just like my ex-wife and, it appears, everyone around me.

I'm worried that I'll never be able trust myself or my own judgment again.

Seventeen

Lyric

I'm nervous. A few weeks ago, before Aruba, my parents put me in contact with an attorney and he found my biological mother, Athena George. He gave me her phone number, but I was too afraid to call her.

I learned that Athena had agreed that when I turned eighteen, I could make contact with her if I wanted to, but I turned eighteen over a decade ago. She could have changed her mind. She could have a different life now and might not want to revisit the mistakes of the past.

But you're not a mistake, my inner voice says.

You can do this. Just pick up the phone, dial the digits and put yourself out of your misery.

I've been agonizing about this for months. However, the trip to Aruba helped me get in touch not only with my sensuality, but with my emotions. I allowed myself to *feel* after holding everything about my parentage and my sense of belonging inside for too long.

I'm ready for this next step. The opening of LT Dance Academy was a success. I have fifteen students, which is pretty darn amazing for a new dance school. I never imagined I would be off to such a good start. I feel different, changed somehow by my experience on the island, and finally contacting my biological mother is the next logical step in making myself feel whole.

It's why I've decided it's time to take the bull by the horns. Before I talk myself out of it, I grab my phone.

"Hello?" A woman answers on the other end.

"Um, Athena George?" I inquire.

"Yes, who is this?"

"I-I…" I stutter; there's no easy way to say it, so I blurt out, "I'm your daughter."

"I don't have…" she begins, but then stops herself. "Omigod!" I can tell when she realizes who I am because suddenly the phone is quiet on the other end.

"Are you still there?" I ask softly.

"Yes, yes, I am. I just—I thought when you didn't reach out to me when you were eighteen… I assumed you didn't want to see me and I closed that chapter in my life. I-I never imagined…" Athena's voice trails off.

"I would call twelve years later?" I offer.

"Something like that."

"I've always known I was adopted. My parents told me when I was five years old. But well, when I found out I could contact you, I guess I needed time to process it," I respond. "Plus, my work schedule at the time was so busy, it didn't leave me much time for a life, but I've moved back here to Memphis and thought it was time." I realize I'm rambling and pause to catch my breath. "Do you still live here?"

"I do."

A sigh of relief escapes my lips. "Would you be willing to meet me?"

"If that's what you want."

But it's not what you want? I push those negative thoughts down. "Yes, I'd like that."

We arrange to meet on Sunday after her church service and I end the call. I can't believe I finally did it. I want to share the big milestone with the Gems, but I'm only able to reach Teagan because the other ladies' phones go straight to voicemail.

"Hey, Lyric." Teagan's bright and smiling face comes up on my screen. "What's going on?"

"Something big, monumental actually, and I had to share it with someone."

Teagan's brow furrows. "Thanks, I think. Did you try calling all the other Gems?"

I chuckle. "I did, and they're all busy it seems."

"Sucks, right? You and I are the only singletons left," Teagan responds.

"Yeah, but today it doesn't matter because I reached out to my birth mother."

"You did?" Shock is evident in Teagan's voice. "I knew you'd been thinking about it for a while, but I thought you'd let it go."

When the Gems were here, we went out to dinner after

the grand opening and I told them about Athena. They encouraged me to reach out to her, but I was scared. I've had a lot of fears and insecurities to battle through. Plus, fear of how she might react to having the daughter she gave up for adoption suddenly contacting her after all these years. Fear of feeling like an outsider, the way I've felt for much of my life after being raised by white parents.

I've never felt like I belong. Not in the Black community who think I'm not Black enough. Nor in the white community because of the color of my skin. It didn't get any better choosing a career where predominantly Caucasian women with slim bodies are the norm. I was shunned as a Black ballerina.

I was right in that Athena was surprised to hear from me, but the conversation was easier than I imagined. None of the things I've feared recently, such as starting over in a new career as a Black business owner and ballet instructor, have been as bad as I feared.

"How did it go?" Teagan asks, interrupting my musings.

"Fine. She was surprised to hear from me since I didn't contact her at eighteen, but she's willing to meet with me."

"That's a win, isn't it?"

I nod. "Absolutely. I was afraid she might turn the other cheek, ya know? But she didn't. I just want to meet her. It's been difficult not really knowing where I come from, who I look like."

"I can't even imagine what you've gone through, Lyric," Teagan replies softly, "You've always made it seem like it was no big deal. I mean, you lucked out when it comes to having the best adoptive parents. The Taylors are the bomb!"

"I couldn't agree with you more. I love Mama and Daddy, but when I look in the mirror, I need to know who is looking back at me."

"Lyric Ann Taylor," Teagan states emphatically. "A beautiful, accomplished ballet dancer and now a business owner. You're more than just the sum of your genetics."

Trust Teagan to cut to the chase and give it to me straight. Wynter's and Shay's approaches would have been a lot softer, but maybe I need some tough love. If anyone can dish it out, it's Teagan.

"Thanks, girlfriend. I'll let you know how it goes."

"Please do," Teagan responds, "and if you need anything. I'm here for you always."

"I know. Love ya." We end the call and I lean back on the couch. I feel better about taking this monumental step. I'll need to tell my parents, but they've always been supportive of this journey and have never once given me the feeling of being jealous of any potential relationship I might have with my birth parents.

And that's because they know I love them and no one can break that bond.

The next day, after showering and changing into leggings, sports bra and a tank, I stop off for a coffee at Starbucks and head into the dance studio to do some admin work. I thought owning my place would be all about the dancing, but I'm quickly realizing so much more is involved. Scheduling, accounting, marketing and social media, and making sure the website is updated to get my name out there—it's all part of the package. It's going to be a full day, too. I have four classes and a private session.

My first class goes quickly with my two- to four-year-olds. I only have four of them, but they are so precious, and I absolutely adore them. Afterward, we play a session of duck duck goose and then I hand them off to their parents, who are watching them right outside the glass.

My 10:00 a.m. class is with students ages four to six years old. I look forward to this class because they're able to follow direction a bit better than my earlier group. I'm especially excited to see Kianna. She's only been to two sessions, but I see a spark in her. She easily catches on to the movements I teach as if she were born to dance.

I step out of the studio for a few minutes to get some water as the students start filling in. I have five students in this class, small enough for me to give all the girls individual instruction. As word gets around, I hope to have some young men in my class, too.

I gobble down a protein bar and guzzle an entire bottle of water in the break room before heading down the corridor, but then my footsteps halt midway because standing in the hallway is none other than Devon Masters.

My heart hammers in my chest uncontrollably and my stomach goes into a free fall. What the hell is he doing *here* in my studio? My memory quickly offers up thoughts of us together. How we fit like pieces of a puzzle. Our hot, damp skin sliding against each other.

He senses my gaze on him because he turns his head and his warm honey-brown eyes widen in surprise when he sees me. At first, he appears happy, but then a coldness takes over his features and I feel ice rushing through my veins. He blinks and then turns away and faces the window of the studio where parents watch their children dancing.

Devon has a child.

A daughter.

Omigod! Which little girl in my class is his?

My timer goes off on my watch with my ten-minute warning telling me class is nearly ready to start. I force my feet to begin walking. I say hello to several parents standing in the corridor. I glance in Devon's direction, wondering if he'll acknowledge my presence. I know he has a low opinion of me. He thinks I'm having an affair with *my father* of all people. He glances up as I walk past him and I give him a curt nod. I won't let his narrow mind get the better of me. I didn't do anything wrong and have nothing to be ashamed of.

I sweep past him and head into the studio where five sets of smiling faces are there to greet me.

"Good morning, girls," I say with a grin. "How's everyone doing today?"

A chorus of "goods" round out the room.

"Excellent. We're going to have lots of fun today."

I tell myself not to look at the window, but I can't help myself, and when I do, I find Devon's gaze is on me, watching my every movement.

Be calm, Lyric.

This is your studio, not his. Don't let him intimidate you.

So I walk over to the mirror to start my session and ignore the pit in my stomach that the man I've dreamed of, fantasized about in the shower, is now here in the flesh.

Eighteen

Devon

What the fuck!

I try to tell myself to calm down, but I can't. Lyric is here in the building. She walked by me and was almost close enough for me to get a whiff of the vanilla and jasmine scent that drove me wild for a week. A scent I can't get out of my head no matter how hard I try. And now I find out she's my daughter's teacher?

I used to enjoy dancing, watching it as well as dancing myself, but Shiloh tainted the pastime as well as my trust and faith.

And now it appears the fates are against me, too.

First, the mix-up at the villa brought me into Lyric's sphere, and now my daughter is taking ballet at her dance studio?

Even more is the reality that Lyric is a dancer just like Shiloh!

I should have known. The way she glided across the club's dance floor in Aruba had me hypnotized. She had a natural flow and rhythm as if her body was made for movement. And it was because she studied it. I can see it in the way she moves now, showing the young girls ballet moves.

Damn it! After the airport, I thought I would never have to see Lyric again. I didn't think I could bear reminders of my vulnerabilities, her lies, but when I saw her standing in the hall looking so ethereal and beautiful, I realized I miss her.

And I hate feeling this way.

She made me want to trust again. When we were in Aruba, I began to let go of past hurts, fears and insecurities. The wall around my heart was coming down, but then I discovered Lyric had someone waiting at home. It hurt because I'd begun to think of Lyric as mine. Like I had some claim on her, which clearly I didn't.

We made a sex pact. What happens in Aruba, stays there. She followed it. I can't be angry at her because she had someone else waiting in the wings. I'm just jealous that bastard gets to have her in his bed. There was a moment there, at the end, when I considered having us continue in the real world....

I close my eyes, but when I open them I see Lyric with Kianna, showing her a dance that my daughter executes flawlessly. Chantel is right. She's good. *Just like her mother.* Why couldn't Kianna have taken after me? Instead, she wants to follow in her mother's footsteps.

I don't know how to handle this. Dance brings up all the bad memories for me. Of Shiloh being late to dinner.

Of Shiloh being gone for days or weeks at a time because she got a gig she couldn't turn down. Of her not wanting to be intimate because she was too tired or too sore after dancing all day. I loved her, but never seemed to have her attention, never seemed to come first. I felt unwanted, unloved, *unseen*.

"Think about what this pregnancy will do to my body," she'd wailed. Maybe I guilted her into becoming a mother? I wanted our child so desperately. I'd wanted a family with her. I wanted forever.

That's back when I still believed in that fairy tale.

"She's amazing, isn't she?" one of the mothers beside me asks.

I'm the only father in attendance at the dance studio. I'm used to it because it's always been just me and Kianna.

"Who's amazing?" I ask, and assume she's talking about her daughter.

"Lyric," the woman states. "She's flawless. I'm so excited to have my daughter study under her. Did you know she was a principal dancer for the San Francisco Ballet? It's the oldest ballet company in the US."

"No, I didn't." I had no idea because Lyric and I didn't get too personal in Aruba. That had been the agreement. We mainly spoke in generalities and stayed on easy subjects. We told each other what we did for a living. She knows I'm a software engineer, and I knew she was opening a new business, but I never asked her what that business was.

We discussed our families and siblings. I knew she was adopted, but we hadn't gotten much deeper than that. How deep would we have gotten if we'd shared more on the island? Perhaps we should have; then I wouldn't still feel this burn even though I barely know her at all.

"Well, our daughters are being taught by the very best. Not many people become principal in a dance company, especially someone like her. If she hadn't been injured, she would have had a long career."

Someone like her? I turn to glare at the woman, stunned by her confession. "And what is that supposed to mean?"

"I-I just meant there's not a lot of African American ballet dancers," the woman ekes out.

I turn to watch Lyric again through the window and have to agree with the woman. The way Lyric elongates her leg on the barre is nothing short of magical. Her body is perfection and I know all the ways she can use it. She made me want her, and now she's all I can think about.

When I'm at work, sometimes, my mind drifts to our time together and I wonder...

Stop it, Devon.

It's over. It has to be. I was already at a deficit in the trust department. And yes, our relationship was physical, but there were moments I saw more. Wanted there to be more. Now she's got me questioning my own judgment.

This feels familiar. I've done this. The lies, the cheating, the dance career. I can't do it again.

The class is only an hour and soon it's over. Kianna walks out a few minutes later looking happier than I've ever seen her.

"Did you see me, Daddy?" Kianna asks excitedly.

"Yes, I did, sweetheart. You were wonderful."

A large smile spreads across Kianna's face, and I can see her dimples, which she gets from me. "Thank you. I had so much fun today. Miss Taylor is so awesome!"

She has no idea who Miss Taylor is to me, and I don't tell her. "Kianna, would you mind waiting out here while I have a word with Miss Taylor?"

"Okay, Daddy." She sits on a nearby bench.

When I walk inside the studio, Lyric's back is to me and she's running a dry mop over the floor. She can see me through the mirror, but chooses to ignore me.

We're both silent for several seconds before she says, "What do you want, Devon?" Her voice is husky, but hearing her say my name again makes my breath jerk.

For a moment, I remember.

Desire pours through me. I want to sweep her into my arms, kiss her...and then I remember reality. She's with another man.

Anger pulses over my skin. "Did you know Kianna was my daughter when you signed her up?" I snap.

She drops the mop and swings around fast to face me. I feel like I have whiplash. Her eyes lock with mine and my heart turns into ice because that's how it felt when I saw her in the arms of that other man.

"And exactly how would I have known that?" she asks, folding her arms across her pert breasts. Breasts my mouth have been on, tasted, sucked so many times I lost count. My dick starts to swell even though I'm angry.

"We didn't exactly tell each other a lot of details about our life, on purpose. When you weren't volunteering anything, I assumed that's the way you wanted it so I kept my mouth shut."

She's right. I want to argue, but I can't.

"Kianna can't come here," I announce.

Her eyes flash with fire, and I can see she's going to fight me on this. "Why not? She's one of my best students, and I know it hasn't been long, but I see such potential in her."

My eyes narrow. "You know why she can't come here."

Her cheeks turn red, and it reminds me of the first time, when I suggested we become lovers for the week. It amazes me that she can pull the trick out at will. "Surely we can get beyond what happened for the sake of your daughter."

"Don't act like you suddenly know Kianna because you've helped her twirl a few times." My words are harsh. I know I'm being completely insensitive, but I don't care. I can't do this. I can't be around Lyric week in and week out and not want to have her fully in my life, even though I know she's with someone else.

It's not good for me or her.

"I never said I did," Lyric responds. "But she likes it here. Look at her." She motions to the door and Kianna has moved from the bench and is staring at us, smiling.

I turn back around and face Lyric. "Don't you dare try to emotionally blackmail me."

"Is that what I'm doing?" Lyric asks, walking closer to me until she's a few inches away and her scent washes over me. "I thought I was fighting to ensure Kianna gets to do something she loves."

If she takes one step closer I swear I'll haul her ass toward me and capture her lips with mine regardless of who's standing outside looking at us. "Don't take another step."

"Or what?" she taunts me, her eyes burning into mine.

"I'm warning you…"

She takes another step toward me, and I'm just about to grab her when the studio door opens. Several young teenage girls start piling in.

"It's time for my next class," Lyric replies with a smirk as if she knew what I'd been planning to do.

My eyes narrow. "This isn't over, Lyric."

"I didn't think it was."

I give her one long stare, which she gives right back to me, then I turn on my heel and walk out. Kianna is waiting for me and Lyric has students. This just means we need to have a discussion *in private* where no one can hear us— then I can finally tell Lyric exactly what I think of her and that going forward, Kianna will no longer be her student. Not if I have anything to say about it.

Nineteen

Lyric

I'm thankful when my last class of the day is over, when I can lock the door and finally allow the impact of seeing Devon again wash over me. When I woke up this morning, I didn't know my world would tilt on its axis *again*.

Is it because I still have feelings for Devon that I've refused to give credence to? Ever since we left the island, I've shoved him into the far recesses of my mind. I had so much more to focus on in the interim, like speaking with Athena, the grand opening and getting LT Dance Academy off the ground.

But now there's no hiding behind my family or my work.

Having Devon in my studio was jarring. He looked at me with such contempt. I didn't do anything wrong. It's not my fault he thinks I lied to him. If he chooses to believe the worst of me, without even asking for the truth, so be it. It means he didn't know me at all. But how is that possible when he was closer to me than I've ever allowed any man to be?

When he came into the room to confront me, my entire body went rigid and my pulse raced. I couldn't let him see it, though. So I stood behind my bravado.

It was a shock coming face-to-face with him. He is as absurdly handsome as he was the first time I laid eyes on him on the plane. His thick, deliciously curly fade that I ran my hands through over and over again, that curving sensual mouth he knows how to use to bring me such pleasure, those unyielding brown eyes. When his gaze slammed into mine, I nearly lost myself.

Devon is angry because he thinks I somehow engineered it for his daughter to dance at my school? That's ridiculous. What kind of mistrust and hurt would it take for someone to get to that conclusion? I had no idea who Kianna was. I didn't put her last name and Devon's together. I assumed her mother was the woman who signed her up, Chantel Dixon, but obviously Devon's ex-wife is deceased. Does it matter now? Kianna's a student at the academy, and she likes it here. I would hate for Devon to pull Kianna out because of me. Because he hates me.

But does he?

Standing alone in that studio, I felt the familiar lick of heat between us. The same flame that burned hot in Aruba is still there. I know it and suspect he does, too. I guess that's why I pushed him, taunting him to take action when he told me not to take another step.

He still wants me even though he doesn't want to want

me. I don't want to want him, either, not if he thinks I'm capable of deception, of lying to his face. What happened between us is in the past, and I have to leave it there.

Or at least that's what I tell myself.

Later that evening, I pick up a bowl of ramen filled with pork belly, ginger, seaweed, green onion, bamboo shoots and egg. It's what I've been craving all day and after I indulge, I curl up on the sofa and contact Shay. I didn't tell the Gems what happened in Aruba. So much was going on when they were here, I didn't want to bring down the mood with my short-lived affair, but if anyone can understand, it's Shay.

Shay and Colin's relationship began unconventionally. We all knew one another in high school, but Shay had a huge crush on Colin and he never paid her an ounce of attention. A decade later, they reconnected. Shay started out as Colin's yoga instructor, but things quickly turned heated. They had a purely physical relationship, like Devon and I did, but unlike ours, they ended up together in the end.

I place a video call to Shay, and this time she's free. I see she's still at her yoga studio.

"Hello, darlin'," she says with a Texas drawl.

I laugh. "Hey, girl, I was hoping you had some time to chat?"

"For you? Anytime. What's going on?"

I proceed to fill Shay in on all the details of how Devon and I ended up in the same villa and how the attraction between us exploded. Afterward, Shay stares back at me in disbelief.

"What?" I ask.

"Lyric, you, of all people. I have to say I'm a bit shocked and scandalized, but good for you," Shay responds.

"You're surprised that I could be spontaneous?"

Shay laughs. "Heck, yeah. You've always been a planner and very methodical, but I assumed that came from years of training."

"It did. The thing is, I never expected to like Devon so much."

"Ah, there's the rub, isn't it?" Shay asks. "The same thing happened to me, Lyric. I thought I could handle the physical and not catch feelings, but I fell head over heels for Colin. I'm not sure if we can separate our feelings as easily as we think we can."

"I know, right? But maybe Devon is someone who can. He never once mentioned changing our arrangement, not the entire week on the island. While I…"

"Developed feelings for him?"

I nod. "And here's where our story parallel ends. I thought I'd never see Devon after the airport."

"Where he thought you and your father were lovers." Shay bursts out laughing. "Of all the things I've ever heard, *that* takes the cake. What was he thinking?"

I shrug. "I don't know, but somehow his daughter has found her way to my studio. She's one of my students, Shay."

"Wow! Did you know?"

"Of course not. I was so happy to get students, I didn't make the connection with her last name. Besides, once I had time to review things, I saw Devon didn't sign her up. Her aunt Chantel Dixon did."

"What happened?"

"Devon confronted me after class and accused me of setting up the entire scenario, which is far from the truth."

"He leaps to conclusions an awful lot."

"Yes, he does." I wonder if he was hurt in the past, maybe by his ex-wife? Maybe that's why he's so quick to jump to the worst conclusions without having all the facts. "I tried to reason with him. Kianna enjoys the class and has promise, but I'm not sure if I got through to him. I suspect he's going to pull her out of the academy and not only will I lose a student, but also a promising dancer might never move forward."

"Maybe once he calms down, cooler heads will prevail."

"I certainly hope so, but in the meantime, I can't deny that when I saw him, my heart lurched. There's still something there, Shay, and that's what is scary."

"It's always scary to put ourselves out there and take a risk," Shay replies, "but if I could give you a piece of advice from what I learned—don't be afraid to go after what you want even if doesn't turn out how you planned it. I mean, look at you, you wanted to become the next Misty Copeland, and you did."

"For a little while."

Shay shook her head. "Doesn't matter, you became a principal in one of the nation's leading dance companies. Give yourself a pat on the back. That was a big accomplishment."

"Thank you, Shay. I'm glad we talked."

"You're welcome. If you need to talk this out any more let me know…in the meantime, a certain accountant has come to my office to pull me away." Suddenly, Colin, Shay's boyfriend, shows his face in my screen and waves just as Shay ends the call.

I'm happy for Shay and maybe just a bit envious. Maybe I could have a love story like hers one day.

I wake up the next morning with knots in my stomach. Not about Devon. I've pushed him aside, at least for now. Today is the day I'm finally meeting my birth mother. I'm so nervous I can't eat and can only drink a bit of coffee.

I spend an extraordinarily long time choosing what to wear for our first meeting. Since it's cold out, I decide on some jeans, a ruched sweater and a long cardigan to go over it. I add a dangling necklace and matching earrings and put my auburn hair into a high ponytail. I'm not much for makeup but because I'm meeting my mother for the first time, I put in a little effort with some powder, mascara and lipstick.

I'm happy with the results and remind myself this is a good thing. Minutes later, I slide behind the wheel and drive to a popular brunch spot in town. I texted Athena a few days ago and told her I would make a reservation in my name. When I arrive, the parking lot is nearly full, but I manage to find a spot in the far back and ease my Toyota Camry into it.

I inhale a few quick deep breaths and exit the vehicle. The sidewalk is littered with people milling about, but I head to the front counter.

"Good afternoon, I have a reservation, Lyric Taylor."

The hostess nods. "Yes, I see your name." She reaches behind her and grabs two paper menus. "Please follow me."

The inside of the restaurant is classic with wood chairs and red upholstery, white linen tablecloths. I wanted to go someplace nice for my first meeting with my biological mother.

I follow behind the hostess, and she seats us in a quiet booth away from the crowd. I made sure to ask for some privacy when I made the reservation and am happy they were able to accommodate me.

I'm super nervous. My hands are clammy and I feel a bead of sweat on my forehead. *Breathe, Lyric. Breathe.* I'm giving myself a pep talk when I look up and see a woman standing in front of me with a rich honey complexion that's very different from my own. She isn't much taller than me, though, maybe a couple of inches. Athena has a short bob with a part down the middle, a round face and almond-shaped eyes—at least that we share. My heart constricts.

"Lyric?"

I nod. Unable to speak.

"I'm Athena."

I force myself to my feet and offer my hand, but instead of shaking it, she awkwardly pulls me into her embrace. The action catches me off guard and I stumble. The hug doesn't last long, but it's long enough to disconcert me. I pull away, embarrassed and a little guilty that I enjoyed it. It feels like a betrayal of sorts to Mama, who encouraged me to meet Athena.

"Let's sit, shall we?" she asks, and we both take a seat at the booth. She stares at me. "You're so pretty. I-I never..."

Her voice trails off and she shakes her head. "I'm sorry. This is all so surreal."

"For me, too," I add.

She snorts. "You're so tiny. I feel like I need to feed you."

I laugh out loud. "I'm a dancer and for many years I was on a very strict diet."

"And now?"

"I can pretty much eat whatever I want without gaining any weight. Good genes, I guess." I say the words without thinking.

Athena is quiet again, so I try to engage her in conversation. "Are you from here?"

"Born and raised." She pauses for a moment as if deep in thought, or maybe my presence is bringing back memories she would rather have stayed in the past?

"I lived here for most of my life," I add, "though my family did move to Texas for several years before returning to Memphis. There's no place like home, right?" I offer her a smile, but I see she's wringing her hands on the table.

"Do you have any family here?" I press on.

I'm determined to get what I came for, which is to know more about where I come from even if she's reluctant to give the information.

"My father is a pastor in the church."

"A pastor." I repeat her words, trying to figure out how to get her to open up. She's sitting across from me with a wary expression. If she didn't want to come, why did she agree to meet with me? Anger starts to boil inside me, but I push it down. I came here for answers and I'm not leaving until I get some. "Did he know about me? I mean, er…"

"Yes, he did. When I became pregnant, well, it was an embarrassment, not to mention disappointing for him."

"I see." My grandfather was embarrassed by my mere existence. "Did he know you gave me up for adoption?"

Athena nods furiously. "It was his suggestion. He never forgave me for getting pregnant. Our relationship changed after that. Even after—after I gave you up. I could never seem to please him, not even when I got my teaching degree."

"You're a teacher?" At least we share something in common.

"Yes. Fourth and fifth grade mostly. Though it's getting harder and harder each year. Kids just aren't the same. And you—what do you do? Oh wait, you told me. You're a dancer."

"I am. Well, I was a ballerina," I amend, "but I recently opened my own dance studio in town. I teach ballet, tap, jazz and contemporary."

"Wow! You're so accomplished. And your parents?"

"The Taylors are amazing. I'm very lucky to have been adopted by such wonderful people."

The waitress finally comes around to take our drink orders, but we both go ahead and order our entrée. I order avocado toast and Athena gets the fried chicken and French toast with maple butter.

"You're sure you don't want more?" Athena asks. "That doesn't seem like enough to eat."

"It's fine." I don't want to tell her that being here has my stomach tied up in knots and I don't have much of an appetite.

Once the waitress has gone, the conversation ceases. It's not like my dinners at home with Mama and Daddy where we can't stop talking about our day and what's going on in our lives. But I asked Athena here today, and I'm not sure if I'll see her again. Or if I'll have the courage to reach out again, or if she'd want me to. So I need to ask the hard questions now, while I have the chance. Find out what I've always wanted to know.

"You were sixteen when you had me?" I start.

She nods. "I fell for one of the neighborhood boys in town who my father warned me to stay away from, but I guess I had a thing for bad boys. When I laid down with him, I thought we were just going to fool around a bit, but then things became heated and, well… I ended up pregnant with you."

I stare back at her, but I have to know more. "Did you tell him, my, er…birth father about me?"

"I did, but he didn't believe me. Said I probably slept with other guys in town. When I told him he was my first he laughed in my face."

I clutch my hand to chest. "I'm so sorry."

Athena shakes her head and an errant tear slides down her cheek. I reach for her hand to comfort her, but she pulls away before I can. I try not to be hurt by her actions, but I am.

"I didn't know what to do," Athena continues. "Eventually Mama realized what was going on when I didn't have a period. She forced me to tell my father. He slapped me across the face and told me he was ashamed of me. Said I had to give you up."

I swallow the lump in my throat. "So there was never any thought of keeping me?" My voice is quiet, but I've always wanted to know if that was ever a consideration, if she *wanted* me.

"I'm sorry, but no." She shakes her head. "My parents were adamant I give the baby up and arranged the adoption. I went to live with my aunt on the other side of the town until I had you."

Hearing the story of how I was conceived and born is disheartening. I don't know what I expected. Maybe there was some hope in the back of my mind that Athena *wanted* to keep me, but instead it's very cut-and-dried. She slept with a bad boy, wound up pregnant and gave me up for adoption. Simple as that.

The waitress returns with our food and Athena eats her meal while I can only manage a few bites. I've lost my appetite.

"I held you, once," Athena says, cutting into my thoughts as she cuts her French toast, "when you were born. I didn't want to, but the nurse said I would always regret it if I didn't. I knew I couldn't give you the life you deserved. I did the right thing. I gave you to people who would love and care for you."

Tears slide down my cheeks at her words and I nod. What can I do? Athena doesn't feel any remorse for letting me go. She feels justified that she was doing what was best, but it hurts nonetheless. "Did you ever wonder about me?"

"Of course I did." *Past tense.* "Every year on your birthday, I wondered if you were okay. My mother told me you went to a good family and I held on to that."

The conversation is pretty much stilted after that, as if Athena has said everything she needs to say. I feel gutted by her words so I remain silent. I don't know what I was hoping for. That she would take me in her arms and admit she should never have given me up and it was the biggest regret of her life? Maybe. I just didn't expect her to be so detached. I need more time to process the jumble of emotions that I'm feeling at how this lunch turned out. It's only when the bill comes and she reaches for it that we speak again.

"It's the least I can do," Athena responds.

So I ask her my final question. "Who is my father?"

Twenty

Lyric

I can tell Athena doesn't like my question by the frown that mars her round face. "Why do you need to know?"

"Because I do," I respond hotly. I've listened to everything she had to say. Now it's my turn.

"It won't change anything," Athena replies. "You have two wonderful parents who love you. Surely you can put this to bed now that we've met?"

I shake my head furiously. "I'm sorry, but I can't. I want to know who my father is. I deserve to know. And besides, I want my complete medical history. I need to know if there's anything that may come back and bite me later in life. *Please*." I add the last word and can see Athena's mind working out a way to get around giving me the truth.

In the end, however, she sighs heavily and places her hands on the table. "His name is Jeremy Duncan."

"The famous record producer?" I inquire.

She nods.

"I…" I'm stunned. I've heard of him. Who hasn't? He's extremely popular in town, but I never dreamed he was my birth father.

"I warn you he won't believe you," Athena responds. "He didn't believe me then, and I doubt he'll believe you now."

"Understood and thank you. I know it wasn't easy coming here and meeting me today, telling me your story, but I appreciate you doing so."

"Of course. As you say, I owed you."

I hate that Athena feels that way. I would have hoped she would have *wanted* to see me, get to know me, but I was deluding myself. I guess the young girl inside me just wanted to be loved.

We say our goodbyes and this time, Athena doesn't bother to hug me. I watch her leave the restaurant and then sit back in the booth, unable to hold back the tears that fall down my cheeks.

I took a risk meeting her because I felt renewed after the Aruba trip and ready to take on anything. I hoped she would embrace me, and I would no longer feel like an outsider the way I have most of my life. I've never fit in the Black community, white neighborhood or body-conscious ballet world. My parents did their best to shield and protect me, but they couldn't stop the racism I faced on a day-to-day basis or give me that sense of belonging.

Yet my risk didn't pay off.

I met my birth mother and she doesn't want me now any more than she wanted me back then. That's a bitter pill to swallow.

★ ★ ★

When Monday arrives, I'm not ready for the week.

Yesterday was brutal. Meeting my birth mother gutted me. All I could do was go home to my parents where Mama cuddled me to her bosom and told me she loved me and would always be there for me. I needed that. I didn't realize how much I needed to hear those words. Needed to feel loved.

Mama and Daddy have always done that. Made me feel special even though I'm not their flesh and blood. I thought I would feel differently meeting Athena in person. Thought I would feel some sort of emotional connection. But instead I felt *nothing*. I felt empty and alone.

It was a sobering reality check.

It also killed the childhood dreams I've carried since I was five years old and my parents first told me I was adopted. Just like in a fairy tale, the young girl inside me thought my birth mother loved me but was separated and just couldn't get to me. That wasn't the case. She readily handed me over because I didn't fit into her life or my grandparents' lives. I was an embarrassment and cause of shame, so they washed their hands of me.

I keep replaying the lunch over and over in my head, trying to see if I missed something or misunderstood, but I didn't. Athena isn't interested in a relationship with me. She didn't ask to see me again. She just wanted to close this chapter in her life. Now that it's done, she can move on.

But I can't.

I have to deal with all the revelations she dropped on me, including the fact that my father is some famous producer who doesn't even know he has a daughter out there. I looked him up online and, unlike Athena, he has fair skin like I do. He's very thin, and I imagine I get my figure from him because Athena had big breasts and a round ass, while I have neither. Of course, dance played a large role in my figure, too.

I don't have the energy to think about my biological dad right now, not on the heels of what happened with Athena. Instead, I focus on what I can control, my business.

My mind is whirling as I try to think about what I need to do for the studio. I've come to realize I won't be able to teach every class on my own. I'll wear myself out attempting it. Last week, I put out online advertisements through all my social circles that I'm looking for a dance instructor. I don't have many connections, but when I stopped by my parents' last night, they agreed to tell their friends and church members.

When the bell rings signaling someone's in the lobby, I assume it's probably an instructor candidate, but it's not.

Standing in the middle of my lobby is Devon. What is he doing here? We don't have an appointment. Besides, I'm not ready to deal with him yet. After my disappointing weekend meeting my birth mother, I need time to recoup and deal with the loss I didn't know I would feel after her indifference.

Devon doesn't see me yet, so I watch him peruse my wall of accomplishments. It's my studio, so why not have a brag wall? I have certificates from some of my big wins, like the Youth America Grand Prix and my scholarship certificate to Juilliard, along with pictures of me throughout the years, including when I was a principal dancer for the San Francisco Ballet Company.

"See something that interests you?" I ask, walking toward him.

Devon's eyes grow large at having been caught reading up on me. But then his gaze fixes on me and he treats me to an intense look from the bottom of my sneakered feet to the leggings and tank top I'm wearing before his eyes finally reach mine.

"Lyric."

"Devon."

"Are we alone?" he asks.

I glance around me. "What do you think?"

"Good. I would like to speak with you in private with no interruptions."

"I'm busy. I don't have time to talk." I spin on my heel and head to my office. I'm in no mood for Devon today. Yesterday was emotional, and I'm still recovering from it.

"Well, you're going to make time," Devon replies, and I hear his footsteps as he follows behind me.

I walk behind my desk and when I glance up, he's in my office, filling the space and making me feel small. I try not to think about how this man can unravel me with a single touch. Or how my body still aches for him.

"Fine. You came here for a reason, so let's have it." I forgo any preamble and get right down to business.

"I'm canceling Kianna's enrollment," Devon replies. "I can't have her taught by a woman who lies and cheats."

That makes me snap. "How dare you? You don't know the first thing about me."

His eyes narrowed. "I dare because I *saw* you, Lyric. I saw you with the man at the airport after you told me there was no one else. 'There's no one but you,'" he imitates my voice and it grates on my nerves.

"You're mistaken."

"Are you honestly going to stand there and lie to me again when I saw you with my own eyes?"

I move from around my desk until I'm in front of Devon and he's looking down on me with those accusing eyes.

"That man you saw me with is my *father*."

"You're lying."

I reach behind me to the picture sitting on my desk and shove it into his chest. "Those are my parents, you dimwit. I told you I was adopted, or is a Black girl like me not able to have white parents?"

Devon's face crumples, and I can see all the hot air dissipate from him as if he's a balloon that's been pricked. "But..." He starts, but then stops.

The evidence is right there with me, Mama and Daddy standing in front of the San Francisco Ballet when I was a principal dancer. I fold my arms across my chest and wait. Wait for the apology I'm due.

Devon plops down in the visitor chair and stares at the picture. Finally, he looks at me and I see regret in his eyes. "I'm sorry, Lyric. I owe you an apology. I guess—I leaped to the wrong conclusion when I saw you with your father."

"Yes, you did. I saw you that day and the way you looked at me. I know what you thought."

"But you didn't stop...you let me think..."

"Why would I stop you? It was over between us, so if you wanted to think bad of me, it didn't matter."

"It mattered to me," Devon replies harshly. "I painted you with the same brush as Shi—" He stops what he'd been about to say and scrubs his beard. "Anyway, I'm sorry. I was wrong about you and I can admit that."

I sigh. "I'm glad we got that out of the way. Now, if that's all, I have a lot to do today." I start to move, but then Devon grasps my hand, holding me captive. Electricity shoots through me and I quickly snatch my hand back, bumping my behind against the front of my desk.

Devon stands and studies me. His eyes are so intense. He's so close I can see his irises darken. The air quivers between us like some sort of force field and I can feel his heat and energy humming from beneath his clothes. "Kianna can't stay here."

"Why not?" I glance at him underneath my lashes. "I already kiboshed your misconception about me. There's no reason for her not to stay."

Devon chuckles softly and it lightens the mood. The hostility coming from him has shifted. I find my anger has vanished now, too, leaving me wanting to forgive him and move on even though he's been a complete and utter ass.

He reaches out a hand and brushes his thumb across my lips. I tremble underneath his touch.

"Isn't there?"

I shake my head because I can't think. All thought has stopped, and the room is silent with awareness. Awareness of Devon and my body's reaction toward him.

I start to speak, but Devon is bending his head and covering his mouth with mine, just as he once did in Aruba. I dissolve under the melting heat. He sweeps his tongue over my lips, demanding access, and I open for him, desperate for him like he's some sort of potent drug.

My breath catches when his hands slide to my waist and he draws me closer. Instinctively, I reach for the hard, smooth muscles of his shoulders to hold on to. He pushes me backward until my ass is up against my desk. He steps in between my legs and deepens the kiss, back and forth, fusing our mouths together until I can feel the hardness of his dick pressed against me.

Flickers of heat skate down my limbs, especially when his lips leave mine to find the hollow at the base of my throat and he sucks. He knows that's my spot, and I moan shamelessly, rubbing myself against his dick.

If it wasn't for the shrill of the phone ringing, I'm certain Devon would be taking me on the desk like he did the sink of that restaurant in Aruba. But the phone does interrupt us, and Devon stumbles backward, away from me, gripping the back of my chair as he breathes unsteadily, his eyes ablaze with fire. I stare back at him in bewilderment because heat is pooling in my pelvis and my heart is running wild.

"We shouldn't have done that," he finally says hoarsely.

Despite how angry I am with him, I wanted his kiss. I kissed him back, but his words sting.

"Maybe not, but what's done is done."

"It's why I can't have Kianna here. If she's here, I—I…" He doesn't finish that sentence, but I get the drift.

"I don't think she should be punished because we can't keep our hands off each other."

Devon smiles at my words.

"Listen, I see something in Kianna. She's a natural in ballet. Who knows how far she can go? I can keep a professional distance and treat you and Kianna like any other student and parent. I think she has a real talent, and although there are other dance studios in town, I have been a principal dancer in a major company. I know what it takes if Kianna goes down this path. Let me guide her."

Devon stares at me for several minutes and I think he's going to say no, but he surprises me. "All right, but what just happened, we can't let it happen again."

I agree. We meant to leave it all behind in Aruba, but my need to be loved, to belong, somehow keeps pushing me toward Devon. After what happened with Athena, I'm too vulnerable right now to make good decisions. Plus, I want Kianna to have the same advantages I did. Having someone like Aleksandr as my teacher changed my world.

"Agreed. It will be business and nothing more." I offer my hand and Devon reluctantly shakes it.

Sparks still fly between us but this time I don't act on them. Instead, I watch the man who awakened my dormant sexuality walk away from me.

Again.

Twenty-One

Devon

I stride out of the LT Dance Academy and into the bright sunshine of another Memphis afternoon annoyed by my complete lack of self-control.

When I reach my car and climb inside, I berate myself. What was I thinking?

I'm not. Lyric has a way of getting under my skin, under my defenses. All it takes is one touch and I'm thirsty for her. My jaw clenches tight, and for a few moments I can still feel her lithe body pressed against mine.

It's only been a month but it feels as if it was yesterday that I had unfettered access to her. Lyric knows how to bring me to my knees, and she did today. She showed me she has a power over me that I've not allowed another woman to have in a long time.

It's why I have to keep my distance.

I agreed to allow Kianna to stay at Lyric's school because she told me Kianna has talent. Kianna would be guided by a gifted professional dancer. Maybe I should let her follow this dream?

Chanel is right; I have been letting my issues with dancing get in the way of what's right for my daughter. And honestly, never seeing Lyric again is out of the question. As it is, I feel bad enough for having judged her so harshly. I thought she was sleeping with *her father*!

Christ! I was so jealous when I thought she had moved on to another man after what we shared in Aruba that it skewed my judgment. See? That's what Lyric does to me. She makes me lose all common sense. I came here today to end this once and for all, and now I'm afraid I've made it worse. I want her more than I've ever wanted anything or anyone, including my ex.

I don't know what to do with these feelings in the real world, outside of Aruba. I haven't felt this way in such a long time. Never thought I would ever feel these emotions again. Yet I want to give Kianna this opportunity because it will make my daughter happy, and I'll do anything for Kiana.

My vow is easier said than done. The next couple of weeks go by with Lyric and I both determined to keep our distance. When I bring Kianna to class on Saturdays, I take off her coat and allow her to go into the studio without saying a word to Lyric. Afterward, Lyric gives me a nod of acknowledgment and I do the same.

We act like strangers who never knew each other or each other's bodies, but it's a lie. I know Lyric and how she likes it when I suck on the hollow of her throat. I know how to make her come with my fingers, my tongue or both. But I'm supposed to act as if I don't, even though it kills me to see her in her revealing work outfits. The leotards she wears stick to her slender curves and all I want to do is bury myself in her.

After class, I head to Chantel's. She asked me to pick up Aniya and take her and Kianna to class because she had a hair appointment. It's nice to do something for my sister since she's always looking out for me and Kianna. Being a single father isn't easy, and I couldn't do it without her.

The girls and I stop for pizza along the way and bring it back to the house. I'm setting the lunch at the table and getting them some drinks when Chantel walks in. She's sporting black braids that reach her bottom.

"Wow!" Chantel says. "What's gotten into you?"

I shrug. "I'm helping out by feeding the girls. Can't I do something nice for my sister?"

"You can," Chantel responds. "I'm just surprised you're embracing this ballet dad thing."

I roll my eyes. "Don't remind me." I'm still not a fan of Kianna taking on this extracurricular activity, but I'm trying to be open-minded. And I can't deny she loves it and appears to be pretty good at. A couple of the other moms pointed out Kianna has a natural grace. I guess that's a good thing.

"C'mon, admit it, you're starting to enjoy seeing little girls in tutus," Chantel says with a laugh.

"Ha, ha," I respond. "Want a slice of pizza?"

"I'll take the pizza along with a bottle of beer," Chantel says, moving to her refrigerator. "You care for one?"

"Love one." She unscrews a bottle and hands it to me and we watch the kids dive into the pizza. I take a swig of my beer.

"So." Chantel leans back against the counter. "Kianna tells me you know her teacher, Ms. Taylor."

I nearly choke on the beer and Chantel has to pat my back. "Are you okay, Devo?"

I cough several times. "Uh, sure. Yeah, I'm fine, you just surprised me is all."

"Hmm, did I?" she asks, staring at me suspiciously.

I turn to look at her. "Of course. I don't know why you would think we know each other."

Chantel shrugs. "Kianna said you were talking very 'closely.'" She uses her fingers to make air quotation marks.

I laugh wryly. "You know, kids…"

"Are you really not going to tell me what's going on?" Chantel asks, putting her hands on her hips. "Do I really have to drag this out of you?

I sigh and pull Chantel's sleeve and move us out onto the back porch away from little ears. I take another swig of beer and lean against the banister. "Lyric and I met in Aruba."

Chantel snaps her fingers. "I knew it! I knew something went down in Aruba. You came back all tense when you went there to chill the fuck out. So what happened?"

"I did relax."

She gives me a disbelieving look.

"I did. We did. Lyric and I. And, well, that turned into more and we spent the entire week together."

"Did you now?" Chantel smiles knowingly. "It must be cool being single. I miss the days of having a vacation fling."

"That's what it was supposed to be," I respond. "What happens in Aruba, stays in Aruba, but then *you*,—" I point to Chantel "—enroll my daughter in Lyric's school without my permission. My daughter falls in love with it so then I would look like a complete ogre if I un-enroll her."

Chantel smiles. "There's always other schools. You could have switched her."

And there is the rub. "Kianna likes Lyric."

"You mean, Miss Taylor?" Chantel asks with a knowing grin. "I think it's not who Kianna likes, but who her father likes."

"So what if I do?"

"Exactly." Chantel's dark brown eyes peer into mine. "If you want to be with Lyric, then go for it. Who's stopping you?"

"It's complicated and could get messy if things go sour. It already did. After the trip, I thought Lyric's father was her man when he picked her up at the airport."

Chantel burst out laughing and sprays me with the beer she'd been drinking. "You thought what?"

I shake my head. "I know. I'm an idiot. You don't need to rub it in. I admit I got jealous when I saw her embrace another man and I jumped to conclusions."

"Because you like her more than you're willing to admit. It's okay, Devon, to date again, to let someone in. It didn't work out with Shiloh, but every woman isn't her. You can be happy again. You just have to be willing to allow it."

"It doesn't matter. I already told Lyric I don't want to be with her—that what we had in Aruba was just temporary."

"And exactly when did you tell her this? And how did this conversation come about?"

Why did I open my big mouth? My sister is no fool and instantly caught my slip of the tongue.

"Well?" Chantel folds her arm across her chest. "I'm waiting."

I sigh. She's not going to let this go, so I fess up. "Once I realized Lyric was Kianna's teacher, I went by to see her, to tell her Kianna couldn't stay there. And…"

"And?"

"We kissed," I respond. "Correction. We made out and then I told her it couldn't happen again. She agreed. It's for the best, and we've kept our distance ever since."

"The best for whom? Certainly not the two of you if you can't seem to keep your hands off each other."

"I don't know, Chantel."

"Know what?"

"If I can go there."

"Is Lyric trying to put a ring on your finger or something?"

I laugh out loud. "Well, no, but I don't want her to have expectations. I'm not interested in getting serious with anyone *ever*. I'm not getting married again. That ship has sailed, and I wouldn't want to lead her on that we could be more than lovers."

"And she might be okay with that, but you can't go making these decisions for her without at least discussing it."

"I hear you."

Chantel has given me a lot to think about. I have seen Lyric give me sidelong glances when she thinks I'm not looking. How do I know this? Because I've been doing the very same thing. Being with Lyric excites me and makes me feel more alive than I have in years. I watch her behind the window with her students, I see how she smiles at them. I want her to smile at me like she used to.

Maybe there is a chance we can start again, with all our cards on the table.

I'm not sure what that looks like, but I'll never know until I talk to her.

Twenty-Two

Lyric

"That's right, girls, it's time for our warm-up," I say. We have a routine I put them through where they clap their hands together, then move their heads side to side, lift their shoulders, squeeze their hands and feet, and shake them all around. That seems to relax my young students and get them focused, and they like it because I have a cute accompanying song.

After our warm-up, I clap my hands to get their attention. Bless their hearts, five- and six-year-olds don't have long attention spans either. "It's time to get into first position. Remember you put your heels together and turn your toes out." I wait for them to mimic my movement. "Now, grab a big bouquet of flowers and put it below your belly button."

"Good job." I give them encouragement as they all get into position. "Now we're going to practice our tendu.

That's where you point your toe out to the corner and pull it back in again. Let's try it. Slide to the tippy top of your toe and bring your heel back again so they're together."

Each of the girls seems to remember the instruction from last week.

"Okay, let's try it four times." I hold up my fingers to show the number.

"One and in, two and in, three and in, four and in. Let's give ourselves a high five." I go around the room and give each of the girls a clap.

Then I head back to the front of the room. "Ready for our next move?"

"Yes!" they chorus.

"Our second move will be a plié, which means to bend. So let's go back to first position," Once again, I show them my two heels together and my toes out. "You're going to grab those flowers again, ensure your heels are nice and tight together. Now we're going to make a diamond shape with our legs. With your knees open wide, I want you to sink down just a little bit and then straighten up."

When my students try it, I notice one of them takes her heel off the ground. "Remember, girls, we must keep our heels glued tight to the ground in a plié. So let's try it again. Plié and straight. Plié and straight."

I'm so proud to see each of my students completing the movements to the best of their abilities after barely two months.

"Now let's go on to our third move. From first position with your arms holding your flowers, you go to relevé, which means to rise. So I want you to rise up on your tippy toes, pull your belly button all the way in and then take your heels back down to the ground."

I show them the move and then ask them to duplicate it. "We're going to try that. Relevé up and back down. Up relevé. Hold it. Hold it up as long as you can." I notice some of the girls wobble and fall. "It's okay," I respond, coming to their aid. "We all fall sometime, but you're a big girl when you can get back up."

I receive several wide smiles as they all attempt the action. Afterward, I ask. "How do you feel?"

"Good," they chorus again.

"All right, we're going to try a bourrée turn. To do this, you stand up onto relevé, on your tippy toes, and pull your bellies in nice and tight. Put your arms above your head and then take tiny little steps with your feet until you do a big circle and come back to your first position. Watch me." I simulate the move.

"If you need help balancing, grab your waist." I hold my waist as I practice the move again.

"Let's try it. Up on your toes and relevé. Take tiny little tiptoe steps all around and come back down." The girls mimic my movements.

"Very good. You guys are doing great." I clap my hands to give them encouragement. Once they've practiced a few moves, I have them put it all together with four tendus, two plies, one relevé and one bourrée turn.

A few of the girls catch on, but some don't. I glance over to the window and see a few smiling parents and a few frowns, but I continue my work. We practice several more times, until I feel the girls are ready for the movements with music. I grab the remote.

"All right, we're going to have a little fun with this and have some music."

"Yay!" Kianna claps her hands enthusiastically. She got the combo on the first try, and then helped the other girls in the class practice.

I click the play button and classical ballet music wafts through the air. I get in front of the girls and show them how to put their toes out and back again with four tendus, make diamond shapes with two pliés, rise to their feet on a relevé and do a bourrée turn on their tippy toes.

Afterward, I clap my hands with glee. "Great job. I'm so proud of you."

I really am. I've been pushing them to learn a little bit more each week and they are getting better each time. I end the class with a hint of what's coming. "Next week, we're going to learn second position, the chassé and arabesque."

"Are you all ready for a treat?" I inquire. The girls eagerly nod their heads. That's when my mom comes in with the small ice cream cups. I promised my students if they did well in class, they would be rewarded.

Mama hands the girls each a cup and spoon and they sit on the floor, chatting among themselves and eating their sweet treat. "Thank you for the ice cream, Miss Taylor," Kianna says, coming to me afterward.

"You're welcome, sweetheart," I respond.

"I really like your class."

"I'm glad."

"Could you teach me some of next week's moves?" Kianna inquires.

"I—I..."

"She's very eager," a deep masculine voice states, and I glance up to see Devon has walked into the studio.

"She's just finishing up," I reply quickly.

He laughs. "It's fine. Go enjoy your ice cream, Kianna, while I talk to your teacher."

"Yes, Daddy." Kianna rushes off and plops down on the floor in the back of the studio with the rest of the girls and licks sticky chocolate ice cream from her fingers.

"She's precious." The words fly out of my mouth.

"Yes, she is," Devon replies, and I glance up to find his stunning eyes smoldering. His intense gaze is on me. My tummy flips and every inch of me pulls taut.

"Was there something else?" I'm not sure what Devon is doing in here. He's the one who told me we should keep our distance and I've been doing that, but he's breaking the rules like he did a few weeks ago when he kissed me.

"I'd like to talk to you."

I glance around the room and smile, trying not to give away our conversation to the other parents standing in the back of the room. "After last time, I don't think that's a good idea."

"Maybe not, but I needed to see you," he whispers.

"Pardon?" I give him a sideward glance because surely I didn't hear him correctly.

"You heard me. I just texted you, so send me your address."

I gave Devon my phone number when we were in Aruba,

but he never used it. I assumed after the fiasco at the airport
he deleted me as a contact.

"I will do no such thing," I hiss back all the while trying
to keep a smile on my face and act like I'm having a normal
conversation with a parent.

"You can make a production out of this or you can just
do as I ask."

My eyes narrow. "You're not the boss of me."

"Hmm… I think you rather liked it when I took charge
in the bedroom."

His words are incendiary and my eyes widen with surprise, but he's already walking away and grabbing Kianna's
hand, leading her toward the door. He seems unfazed, but
then he gives himself away by turning around and giving
me a dazzling smile before leaving the studio.

I don't know what to make of that encounter. I mean
Devon is always altering the rules. One minute he's hot,
the next he's cold. He has my head going in circles. Right
when I think I know how to handle him, he changes the
game.

I need to have it out with him once and for all, but I
agree my place of business is not the right setting. When
I'm finally able to get to my office after class, I see Devon's
text. Reluctantly, I send him my address.

His reply is immediate, as if he was waiting for my response. I will be there at six p.m.

He seems to think he runs the show and can tell me how
things are going to be. Maybe on the island that worked.
It was another time, another place. But not now. I have a
voice, and I'm going to tell him exactly how I feel.

★ ★ ★

My tough stance was easier when I was riled up. Now that it's getting closer to six, I find myself on pins and needles.

It's been difficult to ignore Devon since he's reentered my life. In Aruba, we were as intimate as two people can get. We shared an undeniable chemistry. I felt alive and completely uninhibited when I was with him. The things we did together and to each other, I don't know if I would have ever felt comfortable doing them without the right partner. I am thankful for that time of self-discovery.

Is that why I find myself rummaging through my closet to find something to wear? I don't want it to look like I'm trying too hard, but I also want to look my best.

After a quick shower, I put on a casual heather-gray loungewear set of scoop-neck tank top, wide-leg pants and a long-sleeved cardigan. I twist my hair into a messy topknot, add a few sweeps of powder, a little blush on my cheeks to give me color and some pink lip gloss.

I'm ready in just enough time because the doorbell rings at 6:00 p.m. on the dot. Glancing at my reflection, I'm happy with my appearance and trot down the steps of my town house to open the door.

Devon is on the other side and greets me with a smile. I hate that my stomach does a back flip. Men aren't supposed to be beautiful, but Devon is lean, muscular and magnificent.

"Hello." I open the door and allow him into the foyer.

"Hey." His eyes survey me, taking in my hair, casual clothes and lower until he reaches my painted toenails. "You look nice." His eyes travel back to my face.

"Thanks, but I don't think you came over to give me compliments, so should we get this over with?" I go on the offensive. I'm ready for whatever he throws at me because there's always curveballs.

"I was hoping we could have a drink." Devon holds up a bottle of Cupcake muscatel.

He remembered.

That first night at the resort when he ordered a fancy wine that I knew nothing about, I told him I'd be happy with Riesling or a bottle of muscatel.

"Thanks, I can't resist a good muscatel." I lead him past the open-concept living room and dining room into the kitchen and family room area. He gives the space a once-over before walking to the quartz countertop where I'm pulling out a wine opener, and he places the bottle on the counter.

"I'm curious about your request to meet," I say.

I reach for the wine bottle, but he does, too. My fingers tingle at the electric pulse between us, just from a touch. I immediately let go of the bottle. He smiles because he felt it, too. I step away from the counter, allowing him to open the wine while I retrieve some wineglasses.

Even now after all this time, we're still connected. When I find the glasses, I bring them over to the countertop and am silent while Devon fills them. I'm waiting for him to speak, to say something so I know why he's here.

"Salud." He holds up his glass.

I do the same and take a sip. I allow the flavor of the grapes to burst on my tongue, all the while watching him and wondering what he's up to. I keep my kitchen island between us because I can't be too close to him. His spicy scent drives me wild.

He puts his wineglass down. "I might have spoken prematurely when I said we should keep our distance."

My brows furrow. "I don't understand. What does that mean?"

He turns those deep-set brown eyes on me, with the look that makes my panties damp. "It means I can't stop thinking about you, Lyric."

My breath hisses out because I can't stop thinking about him either, but it doesn't mean *we* should go down that road again, which I suspect is what he's about to say.

"Every time I see you, I want to kiss you, touch you, make you mine again," Devon continues. His words light a fire in me and blood rushes through my veins.

"You can't just come in here and say things like that, Devon."

"Why not?"

"Because you—" I point my index finger in his direction "—laid out the ground rules. If you recall, from day one you made it clear you didn't want to see me once we left Aruba. I didn't do that, you did."

"I know, and I've regretted it ever since."

"The only thing you regret is I'm not at your beck and call to service your needs."

His eyes turn stormy, and his expression shoots to one of irritation. "That's not true. I wasn't the only one having my every fantasy fulfilled."

I blush. "That was then, this is now. You're the father of

one of my students, so anything between us would be inappropriate."

"Who says? We're not breaking any rules. There's no ring on either of our fingers."

"So what? You expect us to just pick up where we left off as if the last couple of months haven't happened?" At his silence, I add, "Fuck you, Devon!"

"That's exactly what I want you to do."

A lump forms in my throat, and I push away from behind the counter. "I think it's best if you leave. You were right the first and second time. What happens in Aruba stays there. We should keep our distance." I reach the door, but before I can open it, Devon places his hand there to stop me.

"C'mon, Lyric. Is that really what you want?"

I spin around to face him. "You don't get to tell me what I want."

"Okay, can I show you?" Devon asks, stepping closer until his hard body is pressed into mine.

Christ, why is he making this more difficult? I'm trying to get over him, but my body betrays me. My nipples pebble beneath my tank top and my panties are drenched.

Devon's eyes lower and seconds later, I feel his thumbs brushing the hard nubs of my nipples. "Your body remembers me," he murmurs.

My face flushes at his words, and at his touch, which turns more demanding as he tweaks the crests between his thumbs. I let out a harsh cry.

He smiles. "I've always liked how responsive you are, but this can only happen if we both want it, Lyric."

I lower my head, but he merely takes his other hand to

lift my chin until I meet his eyes. "Do you want me, Lyric? Do you want my mouth on your nipples?"

I suck in a harsh breath. My heart beats frantically in my chest. He expects things to be easy, the way he wants, but I can't let it. I push against his chest and move away from him, eager for some space.

"You don't get to come to my house and make demands because you've had a change of heart. Because you're horny and you think I'm an easy lay."

Exasperation crosses his features. "That's not what I think, Lyric. I'm here admitting I made a mistake. To apologize because I should have allowed our relationship to take its natural course instead of ending it so abruptly on the island."

His admission takes some of the sting out of my sails. "What do you want from me?"

"To enjoy this however long it lasts," Devon responds.

I glare at him. "Because you don't think it will."

"This lust, this attraction, will burn itself out, and when it does, we'll move on."

"And what about Kianna? What happens to her after we've burned out?"

"We'll have to cross that bridge when we come to it."

"I don't want her to suffer because of what's happening between us," I reply. "She's a good dancer, Devon. Really good. She should learn from the best."

"And that's you?"

"Damn right it is. Misty Copeland might have opened the door, but I walked through it. There aren't many ballerinas that look like me working as a principal with a major dance company." I point to my face.

He smiles. "I like your arrogance."

"I deserve it."

"And you know what else you deserve?"

I fold my arms across my chest to hide my puckered nipples from his brooding gaze.

"To see this to the end. Why are you fighting me? I know you want me."

"Now who's arrogant?" I can't help but laugh. Yet seconds later, I'm not laughing because he's tangled his fingers in my hair as he lowers his head.

His lips capture mine in a kiss of pure possession. He thrusts his tongue deep into my mouth, reacquainting himself with every nook and cranny he's been denied. I melt against his onslaught as I take in all of him—his scent, his taste, the very feel of him against me.

He's right. I do want him, *need* him, to make love to me. My body responds the only way it can—I kiss him back. A low groan escapes his throat, and he anchors me to him. His mouth weaves magic against mine to ensure I'm not going anywhere.

"I missed you," he says hoarsely. Then he's trailing hot kisses down my face to my neck and sucks on *that spot*; I arch my hips in unmistakable invitation.

"I want you, too." The admission is torn from me, but I add a caveat: "If we do this, it has to remain a secret. I don't want parents finding out about us and ruining my reputation."

He frowns. "You really think they would care?"

I chuckle. "You have no idea how ruthless dance moms, ballet included, can get. Yes, it's necessary."

"If that's what it takes to have you then yes, we'll keep our relationship hidden." Devon walks me backward toward the stairs while snatching off the cardigan I'm wearing, but we don't make it up the flight and fall in a clumsy mess of limbs on the stairs.

"We are both prisoners of this desire. I need you." Devon lifts my tank top so he can cup my breasts and take one brown peak and then its twin into his mouth. Shards of exquisite pleasure shoot straight to my sex.

I'm not wearing a bra. Did I secretly do that for Devon because I knew he was coming? "Yes, yes…"

Devon starts dragging down my pants and peeling off the triangle of fabric that's my thong until I'm bare from the waist down. He runs a finger along the seam of my body and I jerk away. I reach for the belt and zipper of his jeans with no skill or finesse. I need him inside me. I yank them and his boxers down in one fell swoop until I see his dick.

God, how I've missed it. He's thick and large and very aroused, a bead of precome already on the head.

I want to take him in my mouth, but Devon says, "Later…" He sources a condom from his pocket and protects us both. Then he returns, lifts my leg over his shoulder and enters me with one savage thrust.

My body is so aroused, I eagerly take all of him. This wildfire between us is insane and I glory in it because my body is made for him. Devon begins moving, slowly at first, but then he increases the tempo and pace, claiming me as he drives me higher toward a climax.

I can feel the thud of his heart in unison with mine. I dig my heels into the stairs, my body arching as the first spasm hits me. My climax rips right through me, but Devon doesn't stop. Instead, his thrusts become faster, his breathing more ragged as he takes me over the edge. I'm poised there for endless seconds, alone, and I wonder if he'll join me, but then he gives one final stroke and sends us both into the abyss.

Twenty-Three

Devon

I'm propped up on one elbow staring down at Lyric's sleeping figure. We're in the bedroom of her town house. Her hair is a beautiful halo on the pillow and her face is serene in repose. When I came here tonight, I had no idea if she would give me another chance. I only hoped she would. She did, but she made me work for it. In the end, even she couldn't deny the passion between us.

I thought my hunger for Lyric had been sated on the island, but it seems as if that was only the amuse-bouche. What is it about this woman that drives me to take her on the stairs like some brute?

Even now, when I should be letting her sleep, I can't help but draw the sheets back and glide my fingertips across her small, firm breasts. I love how her nipples pebble at a look or a touch. They're just enough to fill my mouth and hands. My hands trail lower, past her flat stomach and jutting hip bone from years of being a ballerina, and lower to the thatch of curls between her thighs.

My mouth waters. Earlier, I didn't get to taste her, and I've missed her on my tongue. I slide down the bed until my head is between her thighs. My tongue probes her velvet folds.

Her lashes drift open and she glances down, eyes still dazed with sleep. "Devon?"

"Were you expecting someone else?" I chuckle.

She shakes her head. "I—I thought I was dreaming."

"No dream." I spread her legs wider so I can close my lips around the sensitive nub of her clitoris.

"Christ!" Her back arches off the bed.

"Easy." I place my hand on her stomach and lower her back onto the pillows and allow my tongue to dip in once again. She trembles above me as I use the flat of my tongue against her clit to bring her to an orgasm.

She's still spasming when I don another condom and seat myself between her legs. Entwining my fingers with hers, I hold her hands above her head and thrust deep into her body. Our eyes meet and I start to move, never taking my eyes off her. She has me mesmerized, and we begin to move in unison.

Her lashes flutter closed and she moans softly, bowing her body as I thrust deeper and harder. I can feel her muscles tightening, tensing around me, trying to hold me, but her body shudders helplessly. I find her lips and kiss her, fusing our mouths, and that's enough to make me come and groan her name. "Lyric…"

★ ★ ★

It's late when we finally go in search of food. I'm wearing my boxers, and Lyric has on a robe. We've made love several times, as if we have to make up for lost time. There's been lots of touching, stroking, caressing and kissing. We've reveled in the freedom to enjoy each other's bodies once again.

But now, we are both hungry. We pad downstairs to her kitchen and when I glance in the fridge, there's nothing but a block of cheese, a few vegetables and some almond milk.

Lyric shrugs. "Hey, I don't cook. I never learned because I was always at dance class."

"We can order takeout. What's close by?"

We settle on a late-night spot offering Thai food. Pad thai for her and spicy basil chicken for me. When the food arrives, we eat standing up at the kitchen counter while Lyric tells me stories about students in her class. My job isn't very exciting, but I tell her about the last software development project.

Once we're done eating, there's a moment of silence when the air quivers around us. I don't know if she moves first or I do, but we're kissing. Tongues dueling for supremacy. Then I'm tugging the belt around her waist, loosening it until her robe slips down her shoulders. I press my face to her neck and throat, to her breasts, and lick and nip at her skin. She is exquisite and I want to worship her, but her hand is inside my boxers, stroking the swollen head of my dick.

I bat her hand away but she merely pushes me backward to her couch. I'm at her mercy as she straddles me and pulls down my boxers to release me. I gather her intention and grasp her hips to lift her up. I move her back and forward along the tip of my erection, rubbing her clitoris.

"Condom," she moans.

I hate to break the moment, but my pants are by the door where we left them during our haste on the stairs. I retrieve my spare from my wallet since the rest are upstairs and re-join her on the sofa. We pick up where we left off and I lift her again, guiding her down on top of me.

"God, that feels so good." Her head tips back as if she's offering me her nipples. I accept the offering and take one in my mouth, teasing it with gentle licks and flicks while her body rocks back and forth on my dick.

When she tilts her hips to push down again and take me even deeper, I suck in a sharp breath and pinch her nipples. Before I know it, I'm moving with her, thrusting up to meet her and using my hands as an anchor around her waist.

Her nails dig into my shoulders and I pull her closer until she tenses and lets go. Her entire body twitches and jerks. When she cries out, I lick the sounds from her mouth as I, too, shudder underneath her and fly apart.

She folds into me, clutching my head to her chest, and I fall backward onto the couch, spent and panting yet holding her in my arms.

The rest of the week leaves me feeling anxious.

It's not easy for me to get over to Lyric's. Being a single father doesn't allow for much free time. When I'm not at work, I'm rushing to pick up Kianna, making dinner, doing laundry or checking her homework, which isn't much since she's only in the first grade. Because of this new situation-ship with Lyric, sometimes I have to be energetic even when it's hard. I express this to Lyric one night on the phone when I'm lying in bed.

"How long has it been since your ex-wife passed away?" Lyric inquires.

"Three years." I don't want to talk about her with Lyric; hell, not with anyone. It's a time in my life I want to forget other than the precious gift she gave me.

"Kianna was so young. Does she even remember her?"

"No." I shake my head even though she can't see me. "Shiloh wasn't involved in Kianna's life even before the hit-and-run. I had sole custody."

"That's unusual," Lyric replies. "I can't imagine a mother wanting nothing to do with her child."

I grit my teeth. "It happens."

"I would give anything to have a family of my own one day," Lyric responds. "I look forward to being a mother, being there for my children someday."

"Because you were adopted?"

"Partly. I love my parents. They're wonderful and amaz-ing. I couldn't have done any better. But that feeling of truly belonging, having a history, has always felt like it was missing in my life."

"Was it difficult growing up with interracial parents?"

"It was. Kids can be cruel sometimes. They would call me an Oreo. Black on the outside, but white on the inside. They made me feel like I wasn't Black enough. It didn't help that I chose a career dominated by white people. They didn't accept me either. So I've never felt like I belong. When I have a family of my own, maybe then I'll know I belong. That probably sounds silly to you."

I frown. "No, it doesn't. It makes perfect sense. And I hope you find that one day." *But it won't be with me.* I don't say that though I know I should.

Lyric and I haven't discussed the future because we've been so enthralled in the here and now, rediscovering each other. However, from what she's said about family, I know there will come a day when she'll want more. I need to tell her before she gets too invested, but I can't. I know it's selfish to want more time with her, but I do.

"Getting back to Kianna, though," Lyric says, "I can help you out with her, if you want."

"How so?"

"I don't know. I could pick her up sometimes after school or help her with shopping or do her hair."

"You would do that?"

"Sure. I have a lot of flexibility with the studio. I recently hired a part-time teacher to have more time to maintain the administrative side of the business. That's not to say I'm not going to teach, because I love it, especially Kianna's age group. They are so wide-eyed and excited for ballet, like I was at their age."

"Do you miss it?" Unlike Shiloh, Lyric doesn't talk about her ballet days or wax poetic about dancing. In fact, other than that night in Aruba, I haven't even seen her dance. When she's at the studio, she's showing movements, but nothing more.

"Sometimes. I miss the freedom when I was flying

through the air. I felt like a bird, sometimes a swan. But there are other things I don't miss. The constant training. The injuries. And there were always injuries. The average person has no idea the amount of stress ballerinas put on their bodies, not to mention our psyches, trying to live up to an ideal."

"Yet you did it. You reached the mountaintop."

"It wasn't without its challenges, but sometimes yes, I miss dance."

"Then why don't you dance for yourself?" I inquire.

"There isn't time."

I don't believe that. Something is holding her back, but she's too afraid or doesn't want to tell me. That's okay. There's always tomorrow. Maybe we'll both be ready to open up then.

"About this weekend, my sister Chantel is taking the kids up to her in-laws' in Nashville. It means I'll have the house all to myself."

"Is that a fact?"

"Yes, it is, and I want you naked in my bed all weekend long."

"Well, I do have classes on Saturday, but I can come by after."

"All right."

"Don't sulk."

I will try not to. I wanted Lyric in my bed at night and all the hours in between. I like waking up to her sweet smile in the morning. I like the softness of her hair on my pillow and her sweet vanilla and jasmine scent.

I know I'm getting in too deep. I know that intuitively, but I'm like a man possessed.

I just pray when it is over between us, I can go back to the man I used to be.

Twenty-Four

Lyric

I've been distracted from contacting my biological father.

I've been using LT Dance Academy and Devon as avoidance tactics. Athena never called me after our lunch together, but she did email me the medical history form I asked her to complete so I'm happy about that. I shouldn't be surprised she didn't make contact again, but I would be lying if I didn't admit I'm disappointed. I was hoping Athena would change her mind and want to form a relationship, but she hasn't.

I could talk to Mama and Daddy about it, but I don't want to hurt their feelings or have them think I don't love them, because I do. Instead, I share my disappointment with the Gems during our weekly FaceTime call.

"It's okay to have these feelings," Wynter responds after

I tell her what happened. "It's perfectly natural. After all these years, you had a lot of hopes and expectations."

"That were a complete and utter fantasy," I reply. "Reality certainly didn't live up to them. Other than talking about the adoption and seeing the slight physical resemblances, Athena and I really didn't have much to share."

Always the voice of reason, Teagan inquires, "What did you think might happen?"

"I dunno. I didn't expect us to be mother and daughter, but I thought we could have some sort of relationship, if nothing else a friendship."

"I'm sorry, Lyric, but biology doesn't make her your family," Teagan replies softly. "The Taylors have stood by you and supported you your entire life."

"Are you trying to make me feel guilty?" I snap.

"I'm sure she didn't mean it like that," Shay jumps in. I can see she's still in her workout clothes so I appreciate her taking the call. "Did you, Teagan?"

"Of course not," Teagan responds. "I guess I said that very poorly. I was just pointing out that because she's your blood doesn't mean you have anything in common other than DNA."

"Teagan is right," Egypt responds. "The six of us aren't related, yet I feel like each of you is my sister. And I would kick anyone's butt who messes with you."

"Like Claire Watson?" Shay offers, referring to her boyfriend's ex.

Egypt laughs, "That's right, I was prepared to send that heifer a message."

"Where's Asia?" I ask when I notice she isn't on the call.

"Ryan has been keeping her up at all hours," Wynter chimes in. "She texted me she was going to get some shut-eye."

"I still can't believe she's a mom," I respond.

"It certainly doesn't appear to be easy," Shay adds. "Since I'm Ryan's godmother, I flew to Denver last week to help her and Blake out and let Asia rest. It was exhausting. You don't get more than a few hours of sleep in between the feedings, naps and diaper changes. And Asia doesn't want to get a nanny even though Blake offered."

"That's why I'm not having kids for a long time," Teagan announces. "I'm focusing on my career and making my brokerage one of the most successful in Phoenix."

"You don't want children?" I ask. Like I told Devon, I want a family of my own.

"Maybe someday," Teagan says.

"Since we're on the topic…" Wynter starts, "you should know that Riley and I are trying to get pregnant."

"Get out!" I yell, and there are similar replies through the other end of the phone.

"It's still early days," Wynter replies, and then blushes. "But we're having a lot of fun *practicing*."

"I just bet you are, you naughty minx." Egypt laughs.

"Even though I've been busy with baby making, I haven't forgotten your destination wedding, Egypt. In fact, I think you should consider Sandals. They offer a free wedding and you'd get your honeymoon all wrapped in one. All you have to do is tell them what you want and they'll create it."

"Sounds wonderful to me," Egypt replies.

I listen as the two of them banter back and forth about

wedding details until we end the call. I'm happy Egypt has found Garrett, but it makes me wish Devon and I were going down a similar path. We don't talk about the future. And now that I think about it, when he suggested we resume sleeping together, there was no mention of a long-term commitment.

Let's enjoy each other for however long it lasts, he'd said.

Meaning, he doesn't think it will last—that the passionate chemistry we share is fleeting. For me, it isn't. I've not felt this connected to another human being other than the Gems. But there's also the issue of Kianna being my student and how other parents would feel if they thought I was giving her special treatment. So we've kept our relationship a secret.

In the meantime, I have to decide what to do about my biological father: Jeremy Duncan. It's not going to be easy to contact him. I already looked him up online. He's highly popular, so there will be handlers to prevent me from getting in touch with him. What do I do? Show up and announce I'm his daughter? I can contact him on social media. But does he read his own DMs or are they monitored by a publicist? All these questions run through my mind, but I put them on pause because I'm picking up Kianna from school today.

Devon had to work late so I volunteered to get her. The other instructor was already scheduled to teach today while I did some administrative work. I've had a few more students sign up thanks to word of mouth from other parents. It's gratifying to see LT Dance Academy's business moving in the right direction.

I drive to Kianna's school and get in the carpool line, which is all the way down the street. I had no idea how busy it would be for child pickup. I eventually make it to the front of the line and see Kianna standing with her teacher. I wave as I put the car in Park and exit the vehicle to greet them.

"Hello, I'm Lyric Taylor." I extend my hand to the teacher. It's a bit warmer out than it has been over the last month, but it's still brisk. "I'm here to pick up Kianna. Her father should have called ahead. Hi, Kianna." I smile at the young girl. She's dressed in a big puffy jacket, jeans and sneakers.

"Hi, Miss Taylor," Kianna replies politely, offering me her best toothless smile. A few days ago she lost both her front teeth.

"Yes, he did," replies the older woman with a sprinkle of gray in her hair. "Would you mind showing me your ID?"

"Of course." I pull my driver's license from my wallet in my purse and hand it over.

She peruses the license and hands it back. "Well off you go, Kianna. I'll see you tomorrow."

"Bye, Mrs. Wilson." Kianna waves at her teacher.

"Ready to go?" I ask. Kianna nods and to my surprise grabs my hand as we start walking back to my Camry. She has impeccable manners. Devon has raised a wonderful child. After I buckle her into the back seat, I come around to the driver's side and start the engine. Just as I do, Devon's name displays across my car screen. I answer immediately.

"Hey? Were you able to get Kianna okay? I told her teacher you were coming."

"Yes, she's right here," I respond as I put the vehicle in gear and ease onto the road. "Say hello, Kianna."

"Hi, Daddy!"

"How's Daddy's girl?" The genuine affection in Devon's voice is evident and warms my heart.

"I'm good," Kianna replies. "I can't wait to see you, but I'm excited to hang out with Miss Lyric."

"I'll take good care of her," I say.

"I know you will," Devon responds. "I'll be home later, around six p.m. I'll see you both then." He gave me his address a couple of nights ago when he asked if I could pick up Kianna since he had to work late. The last few weeks we'd been holed up at my town house where other parents couldn't see us.

"Sounds good." I hang up the call and turn to Kianna. "How was school today?"

"It was great. We even did some yoga."

"Sounds like a lot of fun. So what would you like to do?"

"Well." Her small round face spreads into a smile. "I was hoping we could look for some tutus?" she asks hopefully. "Daddy doesn't know what to buy, and I only have the one my aunt bought for me."

I love that Kianna is so into ballet. "Absolutely," I respond. "I know just the place."

"You do?"

I nod. We talk animatedly about the color she wants until we arrive at a store I used to frequent back in the day, before Mama started making my outfits. I can't believe it's still open.

Once we go inside, Kianna's eyes widen at the selection of leotards, tutus, tights and accessories. I select a cart.

"C'mon." I grab her hand. "Let's find you a few new things."

I take her to the rack with all the new leotards, and we search through them until we find the exact pink one Kianna wants. "Can I get this one?" she asks.

I glance at the price tag. It's not too bad, and I want her to have all the tools she needs to further her passion for dance. "Definitely. What's your size?"

We peruse a few more racks and our cart fills up with a variety of items from leotards to tutus to tutu dresses, ballet slippers and pointe shoes as well as tights. I got a little carried away, but Kianna is so excited by all her outfits.

I take her to the dressing room, and she tries on a tutu dress. It's pink with cap sleeves and glitter all over.

"What do you think?" Kianna asks, twirling around to show me her best tendu and plié.

I chuckle. "Excellent. What do you think of the dress?"

"I love it!" She beams excitedly.

"Then it's a definite must."

Kianna tries on a few more pieces. When our shopping session is over, we've settled on a pink glittery tutu dress, a new blue leotard with matching tutu and sparkly gold polka dots, and a pair of ballet shoes.

Kianna is thrilled. "This is so much fun," she states when we're checking out. "It's nice to have a woman around to take me shopping. Daddy tries, but he doesn't always know what to get."

"Well, anytime you need help, you let me know." I finish purchasing the items and we take the large bag and head back to the car.

"Thank you," she responds once I've buckled her in. "It's just sometimes I miss having a mommy like the other kids in my class."

When I glance back at her, her mouth is downturned and her bottom lip quivers. I lean back and pat her thigh. "That has to be really tough."

She nods. "Some of the kids at school make fun of me."

"That's not nice."

I remember what it was like being different in school. Growing up with Caucasian parents when I was African American was a real challenge. I was called Oreo and all kinds of bad names.

Kianna continues talking. She must have a lot on her mind. "They talk about my hair." She smooths her hands over her two ponytails. "Daddy isn't very good at doing it. My titi is helping me learn how to do it myself."

"That's good, and I can always help, too. Try not to let it get you down, Kianna. Sometimes other kids don't know how to talk or react to someone who is different from them. They act out, but there is absolutely nothing wrong with you. Your Daddy loves you enough for you and your mommy."

She looks at me and tears glisten in her big brown eyes. "I know. He's the best Daddy ever."

I grin broadly. "What do you say to some ice cream?" I ask in the hopes of making her feel better.

Kianna nods enthusiastically. "Yes, please."

Ten minutes later, we're pulling into a Menchie's frozen

yogurt. Inside the store, Kianna is excited when she sees all the selections. I pay for our yogurts and receive cups from the cashier. Then we head over to pick our flavors.

Kianna chooses strawberry while I opt for the gourmet tiramisu gelato. Kianna adds gummy bears, rainbow sprinkles and marshmallow sauce. Afterward, we take our yogurts to one of the tables inside.

"How is it?" I ask, even though I know the answer. Kianna is gobbling up the yogurt, which would give me a stomachache if I had her selection.

"It's delicious." She puts a big spoon of yogurt in her mouth.

"Good." I'm glad to see the smile back on her face.

When she talked about how cruel kids can be, it struck a nerve. It's difficult being different in school. I had to learn how to navigate those challenges, as will she.

After we finish our yogurts, we head toward her home. When I pull in, Devon's Mazda CX-5 is already there.

"Daddy's home!" Kianna says excitedly, unbuckling her seat belt. "I can't wait to show him all my new ballet stuff."

She emerges from the passenger seat and waits patiently for me at the back of the vehicle. Once I open the trunk, she quickly grabs her two bags.

"I can carry one!" I say, but Kianna is already rushing up the driveway.

The door to the Tudor-style one-story home opens and Devon is waiting with a smile on his face. He lowers all six feet of himself to the ground and greets Kianna with a warm hug. He bestows me with an intent stare that's charged. Devouring.

Shivering with excitement, I follow Kianna's path to the door.

"Thank you for picking up Kianna," Devon says, rising to his feet.

"My pleasure," I respond, and try not to let his heady male scent take my breath away as it always does.

Energy pulses between us for several beats, and Devon's pupils darken. I wonder if he's thinking about kissing me, but then Kianna is pulling on his hand.

"C'mon, Daddy. I want to show you what Lyric bought me."

Devon raises a brow at me, but follows his daughter. I walk in behind them and close the door. Once inside, Kianna drops her book bag in the foyer and heads to the living room, where she rattles on about our visit to the ballet store. I take a seat on one of two beige sofas while Kianna and Devon sit on the other.

The exterior of their home is beautiful with wooden shingle panels along the windows, while the interior decor is a wonderful mix of modern and contemporary design. The white walls with vaulted ceilings and white beams over a gray-washed stone fireplace are gorgeous. It looks like hardwood floors throughout. I can't wait to see more.

"We had so much fun today, Daddy. We went to the ballet store and look what I got." Kianna pulls out everything.

Devon peers at me. "Lyric, this is quite a bit of gear. You shouldn't have gone to the trouble. I have could have purchased this for Kianna."

I shrug. "I know, but I think she wanted a woman's opinion, right, Kianna?"

Kianna nods her head vigorously. "I love all the sparkles."

"They're beautiful, honey. Why don't you take them up to your room and get washed up for dinner? I brought home some takeout."

"Yes, Daddy." Kianna grabs the two bags and marches up the stairs.

When she's no longer in earshot, Devon turns to me. "Lyric, although I appreciate the sentiment, I'm more than capable of taking care of Kianna."

A lump of ice settles in my stomach. I thought he would be pleased, not upset. "I'm sorry if I overstepped. Kianna seemed so happy to have a woman's opinion other than her aunt's. I didn't see the harm."

Devon sighs and pushes to his feet. He walks over to the mantel, where I notice a picture of a beautiful slender woman with the same complexion as Kianna's standing beside Devon holding a toddler. The little one is Kianna. The woman must be Devon's dead ex.

He turns to me with an agonized expression. "I'm sorry. I'm a bit touchy where Kianna is concerned. It's hard being both parents, and apparently according to my daughter—" he glances towards the stairs "—I'm falling short in that department."

I quickly get to my feet and, without thinking, grab his hand. "It's hard for a little girl," I respond. "Sometimes she wants her mother. And I know I'm not her. Just think of me as a sounding board. She wanted to talk about the difficulties of being motherless and I understood."

"But you were adopted. You have both parents."

"Adopted by a white family. I was different from the

other kids in my class, and they never let me forget it. I'm just saying, I know what it's like being in Kianna's shoes, when you don't fit the mold."

Devon's hand reaches out to caress my face and I feel a quickening deep within me. His gaze drops to my lips, and the air between us thickens.

"Thank you." His head swoops down and his lips claim mine in a soft kiss.

When his tongue slides deep into my mouth, a low moan of appreciation escapes my lips, but then we hear the bounding of little feet coming down the stairs and Devon breaks the kiss.

We agreed Kianna can't know about us.

I don't want her to get confused about what's happening between us, especially when I don't know where I fit into their lives long-term. Devon hasn't expressed anything beyond living in the moment. Kianna already has enough to deal with without wondering what's happening with her Daddy and her teacher.

"I brought some Chinese for dinner," Devon says, moving away from me as Kianna enters the living room. "Would you like to join us, Lyric?"

"I wouldn't want to be an imposition."

"You're not. Join us." There is a pleading in his tone, so I accept.

"Thank you."

It feels good to see this other side of Devon when all I've been exposed to previously is how he is as a lover. I can see he's an even better father. He loves Kianna and dotes over her like my parents do for me. If I wanted to get serious and long-term with anyone, it would be Devon, but he doesn't seem keen on wanting more. I glance over at the mantel with the picture of his wife still on display.

Is he still harboring feelings for his dead wife? Is that why he isn't interested in a long-term relationship? I'm afraid to ask. He's been very touchy about talking about his past so I tread very carefully around the subject. Yet that doesn't stop my curiosity, my desire to know what really happened during his marriage. Is there any way I can change his mind about us developing into something richer, deeper?

I've had feelings for Devon since we left Aruba, but I've kept them hidden. At times, like tonight, seeing how he is with Kianna, I realize being with Devon means I could be missing out on a real, lasting relationship.

I want marriage and commitment like the Gems have found. Can I have that one day with Devon? I guess only time will tell.

Twenty-Five

Devon

While eating dinner, I find myself staring at Lyric. This woman has me bewitched. Can she really be this genuine?

I was surprised when she offered to pick up Kianna from school. Based on my experience with other women, after Shiloh's death, I wondered if her offer was a way to get brownie points, but I won't let my mind go there. I've already made too many assumptions. Not doing it again.

Lyric isn't like anyone I've known.

Shiloh and I didn't share the same ideals or vision of what marriage should be. Consequently, we butted heads often. I felt like we were living two separate lives instead of sharing one. It was unequal. I wanted more than she was prepared to give, leaving me feeling insecure. With Lyric, I already feel like a part of her life, and she's starting to feel like a part of mine.

I see the way she interacts with Kianna. Making a plate for her even though I can do it. It looks like being a caregiver comes as naturally to Lyric as breathing. Selfishly, I've been trying to keep our relationship separate so I can have something for myself, but seeing her with Kianna makes me see how desperately my daughter needs a female figure in her life other than my sister.

I see no reason why Kianna and Lyric can't be friends, but there can't be anything beyond that. I refuse to go down the rabbit hole of marriage or commitment again. I've been there, done that. I know the kind of damage and hurt feelings that can occur when one person's feelings are stronger than the other. And I'm not going to be that vulnerable again. This is just sex.

The best sex of my life.

The thought is startling, and makes me more determined than ever to keep Lyric at arm's length. I reach for a carton of egg fried rice and make myself a plate.

After dinner, the three of us watch one of Kianna's favorite channels on YouTube, ZZ Kids, before it's time for her to go to bed. She has school tomorrow. Lyric is about to leave when Kianna asks if she can stay and help Kianna get ready for bed. Lyric looks at me and I nod, giving her the okay. The two of them climb the stairs. I hear their laughs and giggles from above me and wonder what they're up to. I wash the dishes from dinner and put them in the dishwasher before deciding to find out.

Kianna is in her pajamas and Lyric is brushing her hair and creating a complicated hairstyle that I can in no way mimic tomorrow morning. Thankfully, she wraps Kianna's hair in a scarf and the two of them say their prayers. Then Kianna climbs into bed and hands Lyric a book to read to her. The entire experience unsettles me. Kianna never had this with Shiloh. Yet here is Lyric being a stand-in and doing a phenomenal job.

I quietly back away as Lyric reads the bedtime story and make my way downstairs so it doesn't look as if I'm spying on them. On the sofa having a glass of pinot noir is where Lyric finds me when she returns. I've turned off all the lights and only the living room lamps are on to illuminate the area.

"Would you like some?"

Lyric shakes her head. "No, I should get going. I'm sure you didn't intend for me to stay and take up your whole evening. Thank you for allowing me to spend time with Kianna. She's a special little girl."

My eyes darken as I watch Lyric shifting uncomfortably on her feet. "Yes, she is." I put my wineglass down, rise to my feet and move toward her. "Do you have to leave?"

My blood sizzles in my veins and I want her to stay. I step in and encircle her waist, drawing her closer to me.

Lyric glances upstairs. "I —I…"

"When Kianna goes to sleep, she's down for the night." I take Lyric's hand and lead her to my bedroom, which is thankfully on the first level, giving us the privacy we need.

Lyric doesn't object. Instead she presses all that feminine softness against me and fire roars in my veins. Once inside the master bedroom, I back her up against the door and release her hair from the ponytail she likes to wear and slide my fingers through its silkiness.

Then I cradle the back of her skull and lean in for a kiss. She opens her mouth eagerly, drawing me in and stroking her tongue against mine.

"Are you staying?" I ask again, even though her coming to my bedroom feels like a yes.

"Yes."

"Excellent." I lock the door and my hand slides underneath her shirt as bliss beckons me.

Twenty-Six

Lyric

I stayed the night at Devon's even though I know I shouldn't have, but I was enjoying myself too much to leave. Any time with Devon is a delicious and sinful treat. My sore muscles this morning can attest to it. The sexual hunger Devon awakens in me is delightful. We've been lovers for a month and every time were together, it feels as powerful and wonderful as it did in Aruba.

My body is electrified by the devastating touch of his mouth or fingers. But sometimes like this morning, in sleep, he anchors me and I feel safe and secure. I know it's an illusion but I allow myself to revel in it, as if Devon were mine. And spending time with Kianna is no hardship. The whole situation makes me think about what it will be like when I have a family of my own.

I want that.

That sense of belonging.

But I can't get that from Devon or anyone else. I know I have to dig deep and be secure in myself. However, there are relationships in my life that are undone, questions unspoken, that I have to address.

I need to contact my biological father, but how do I go about it?

On my way home to shower before going to the studio, I call Teagan. She always has a good head on her shoulders and thinks logically, where my conclusions are based on emotion.

"The first thing we should do is hire a private investigator to confirm Athena's story," Teagan states when I tell her I want to contact him.

"She seemed certain he was my father. Said he was the only boy she was with."

"And she's probably right, but let's check all the facts, shall we? That way you can present the unvarnished truth to him with absolute certainty you're his daughter."

"How do I do that?"

"With a private investigator. They'll help you find out the best possible way to get in touch and maybe even get a DNA sample."

"I don't have that kind of money."

"Don't worry. The brokerage is doing fabulous," Teagan responds, "and this is something I can do for you. I know how much this means to you, Lyric."

"I'll pay you back, Teagan. LT Dance Academy is slowly getting in the black."

"Hogwash, this is what sisters do. We have each other's backs."

"Thank you." I give her my best smile and end the call. I'm so lucky to have met the Gems in high school. Having them in my life grounded me, back when my life was all about ballet. They made me see there was a world outside the studio.

Though my life now is so different, they still ground me.

Now my dancing is all about teaching others. Business is starting to pick up as word of mouth gets around the community. I'm thankful because Egypt, Asia and even Shay told me being a business owner would be difficult, but I never realized *how* difficult until I opened LT Dance Academy.

Yet I wouldn't give it up for anything.

Later that evening after teaching several classes, I stop by my parents' house because I want to get their take on meeting my biological father. When I use my key, Mama is on the couch doing cross-stitch while Dad is watching *Jeopardy!*

"Lyric, it's good to see you, honey." Mama rises to give me a kiss on the cheek.

I lean down to give Daddy a quick squeeze.

"I agree with your mama. What brings you by on a work night? Everything okay at the studio?"

"Oh yes." I nod. "Two new kids signed up today. One for tap class and another for ballet."

Mama puts down her needlework and claps her hands. "That's wonderful, Lyric. I'm so proud of you. We both are, aren't we, Brad?"

"Absolutely."

I take a seat next to Mama. "Thank you. I couldn't have done it without both of you. You're constantly passing out flyers to neighbors and your church group."

"Anything we can do to help," Mama replies. "But why do I think your visit isn't a social one? Is there something on your mind?"

I can feel perspiration on my upper lip and my stomach churns. "You guys know I reached out to Athena, my birth mother…"

Mama turns to me. "Yes. And it didn't go as you hoped. I'm sorry about that, sweetheart."

I shrug. "It is what it is."

My father turns down the volume on the television. "You're taking it in stride."

"I can't make her want to have a relationship with me."

"No, you can't," Mama responds.

"But I can find out who my biological father is," I add, and look at both of them for a reaction. When there isn't one, I breathe a sigh of relief. "That doesn't concern you?"

Daddy is the first to speak. "Why should it? We have never denied you the right to know where you come from, Lyric. We have always wanted you to know that no matter what DNA might say, *we're*—" he motions back and forth to him and Mama "—your parents. We love, care about and support you."

Tears brim in my eyes. "Thank you, Daddy."

"No need to thank me, Lyric," he replies, "It's a statement of fact. You've been our daughter since the day we brought you home from the hospital and your mother swaddled you in your great-grandmother's blanket like every other Taylor before you."

"But we understand your desire to know your biological parents," Mama says, patting my knee. "We would never stand in the way of that. If you want to have a relationship with them, we'll champion it because we have a lifetime of memories with you."

"I love you both," I say, and allow the tears on my lashes to fall. "This journey is about me needing to know where I belong, where I come from, and I'm so glad you understand that. But know this, no one could ever replace you."

"Well, that's always good to hear." Mama leans across the short distance between us and pulls me into a hug.

Coming home to my parents where I'm loved unconditionally is exactly what I needed. I appreciate their support and that I'm not letting them down by wanting to get to know my biological parents. It gives me a feeling of peace and comfort knowing that I will never lose their love. It's true what they say. There is no place like home.

On the phone with Devon later, I share Teagan's generous request and Mama and Daddy's support of a relationship with my biological parents.

"Your parents are good people."

I'm back at my town house, in my bedroom, after having dinner with my parents. Although I enjoyed my time at Devon's, I didn't get much sleep. I woke to him peppering me with kisses from my breasts to my belly button, then across to my hip before I felt his morning stubble between my thighs. His eyes held mine before he'd tumbled me into ecstasy.

"They are," I agree, and try not to think about how after my orgasm, I'd wrapped one arm around him and put the other on his butt and urged him to take me. Devon barely had time to get a condom on before he was thrusting deep inside me.

"Lyric?"

"Hmm...?"

"Did you hear me?" Devon asks.

I blink and refocus out of the sensual haze of the memory of our hearts thundering in tandem, our breaths in sync as we shuddered together. "What did you say?"

Devon laughs. "I was talking about my parents and how they are nothing like yours. They've been divorced for a number of years. They're always polite toward each other though they both remarried and constantly fight over who will get Kianna for the weekend."

"How does that make you feel?"

"I hate it," Devon responds. "There's more than enough time for Kianna to spend with both grandparents, but don't try to change the subject. I want to know what you were thinking about just now?"

"This morning." I give a soft, throaty laugh.

"Are you wishing for a repeat?" Devon asks, "because if so, you'd have to come here. It's a school night."

I shake my head. "Oh no, mister. I need some rest. You wore me out."

"Yet you can't stop thinking about me any more than I

can stop thinking about you. I could help you with that, you know, relieve any tension you might have."

"Oh yeah, how's that?"

"All you need is your hand," Devon responds huskily.

A blush forms across my face, which Devon is unable to see and I'm silent, but Devon continues speaking, "C'mon, it can be fun."

"I've never had phone sex."

"There's always a first time," Devon replies. "Allow me to initiate you."

"What's the first step?"

"Are you underneath the covers?" he asks.

"Yes," I lie, but quickly scoot underneath my thick comforter.

"Remove your panties," Devon orders.

Since I'm wearing a sleep shirt it's pretty easy to do as I'm told. I tug my underwear down my legs and toss them on the floor.

"Are you doing the same?" I inquire. If I'm going to do this, so should he.

"Absolutely. I'm right there with you."

"Okay. What's next?"

"I want you to slide your hands down your stomach. Slowly, as if I were doing it to you."

"And?"

"When you come to your pussy, I want you to move your fingers across that pretty seam and ease inside. I want you to finger yourself."

"And do you have your hands around your dick?" I taunt.

"Yeah, baby. I'm stroking my dick just like you would." Devon's voice is hoarse and crackling.

I can't believe I'm doing this, but I roll my fingers around my vagina, allowing the friction and pleasure to build.

"Now, go a little faster, rubbing your fingers over your clit. I want you wet for me, Lyric."

Oh, I am. My folds are slick as I envision Devon between my legs like he was this morning with his tongue and fingers. "Yes, yes…" I moan, but I want him with me, too, so I add, "And my lips are wrapped around your dick as I take you in and out of my mouth."

Devon groans. "God, Lyric. You're amazing. Do you feel me? Do you feel my fingers diving in and out of your dripping pussy?"

"O-oh, oh yes," I cry. I frantically start speeding up the pressure, sliding my fingers in and out of my swollen folds. I continue the relentless rhythm.

Devon's orgasm must be close because I can hear his groans intensify.

"Ah…yes." I'm on the edge, too, but I want him to come with me. "My tongue is stroking you up and down while my hands grip your dick harder and faster. I'm taking you as far back in my mouth as I can. Fuck my mouth, Devon!"

I can't believe I'm doing this, being this audacious.

"Jesus Christ!" He groans louder. "I'm—I'm sucking on your clit. Right there. Right where you want me to be, where you need me. Come for me, Lyric."

I want to tell him, *you first,* but heavens it feels too good as I twirl my fingers deeper inside my pussy. I'm driven by this mad desire Devon brings out of me. My body arches off my bed and my legs start quivering. My orgasm strikes and I yell out his name, "Devon!"

He's right behind me and I hear him growl out my name. "Lyric!"

Several minutes pass as I work to regain my sensibilities. I've just had incredible phone sex with Devon. Hearing his voice in my ear as I bring myself to orgasm was incredibly erotic.

"Are you okay?" he asks quietly.

"Mmm-hmm." I haven't regained the power of speech.

"Don't be embarrassed, Lyric. If I could have been there with you, I would have been."

"I know."

"Do you feel relaxed?" he inquires.

Actually, I do. More relaxed than I'd been earlier today, thinking about making contact with my biological father. Devon took my mind off of it. "Yes, I am."

"Good. Sleep well, Lyric."

We bid each other good-night, but it's a long time before I can go to sleep. I'm too wired after that mind-blowing orgasm. I usually don't touch myself and choose a toy instead, but Devon has me exploring new sides of myself. He has me wanting more, not just of the satisfying and addictive sex, but of him.

I want a relationship with him, to belong to him.

I never expected this to happen, but I fear I've fallen for Devon.

Twenty-Seven

Lyric

Another month has gone by with me working hard at LT Dance Academy. Thanks to recommendations from other parents, I've received an influx of new students. So much so I had to hire a second dance teacher to keep up with the load, but the expansion also means I have more paperwork and more things to keep me busy.

Devon and I are actively seeing each other. Usually once on the weekends if he can get Chantel or one of Kianna's grandparents to take her off his hands. Other times, I come over to his place, and once Kianna is asleep, Devon and I explore each other's bodies until we're both exhausted and fall asleep.

One time Kianna nearly found me in his bedroom when, in our haste the night before, we'd inadvertently forgotten to lock the door. Luckily, I was in the en suite bath, but

Devon had to act quickly and throw my clothes in the closet to prevent Kianna from realizing I was there.

In a perfect world, we would tell his daughter we're dating and see where this goes, but Devon and I are in this strange reality where we're sort of dating, but not really. I come over to the house, spend time with him and Kianna, sometimes he cooks. Once when I attempted dinner, it was an epic fail, so we ordered pizza. We watch television as a family, and just last weekend took Kianna to see a live-action version of one of Disney's animated films. We didn't arrive together and sort of "ran into" each other at the concession stand.

We certainly act like a couple who is dating, but Devon doesn't put that label on it. For some reason, it's important to him that I not get the idea our relationship can lead anywhere. So why have me over? Why allow me a greater role in Kianna's life? I don't understand.

It's like he wants me, but not too much. Heaven forbid he realizes I've fallen for him. I haven't told him because I don't want to give up what we have, even though it's not exactly what I want. Am I thinking I can persuade him to change his mind, help him heal from any past hurts, like the death of his ex-wife? Maybe I am. Or at least that's what Teagan thinks, and she lets me know it during our weekly Gems call.

"Do you think you can get him to change his mind?" Teagan asks, after I spill my guts and confess I have strong feelings for the man. If it is love, I don't say it out aloud;

I'd only say it to Devon, even though I doubt he wishes to hear my words of affection.

"I don't know. Maybe."

"You can't change a man," Teagan replies.

At that comment, several of the Gems interrupt.

"I beg to differ," Wynter responds. "Riley *is* a changed man. If you recall, he didn't want to have a relationship with me either, but look at us now." Wynter holds up the rather large diamond ring on her left hand.

"And Colin certainly wasn't trying to do commitment," Shay adds, "but the more time we spent together, in and out of bed, the less he could deny we had something real. Something undeniable."

"All right, all right." Teagan sighs dramatically and leans back in her chair. It looks to me like she's still in the office, which is no surprise. Teagan is a workaholic. "No need to jump all over me. I haven't met one of these amazing men of my own like you ladies seem to have found in San Antonio."

"Girl, San Antonio is not where it's at," Egypt reflects, snapping her fingers. "Garrett is holding it down here in North Carolina. My man is all that and a bag chips."

"Oh Lord, here we go." Teagan rolls her eyes.

"Can we get back to me?" I jump in. Usually, I'm not so pushy, but my relationship or lack thereof weighs heavily on my mind. "I believe we were talking about me and Devon."

"Good for you, Lyric. Don't let us heffas take all the glory because we all booed up," Asia says. "You have to shoot your shot and if it works out, it's meant to be."

"And if doesn't?" I ask.

Asia shrugs. "Then he's not the man for you, sweetheart. Though I know that's easy for me to say with a husband and baby in tow." She points the phone down to where she has a towel over her chest because Ryan is nursing.

"Asia, really?" Teagan asks annoyed. "We don't need to see all your business."

"I'm covered up," Asia snaps back.

"Ladies," Wynter interrupts. "As Lyric stated, this convo is about her and Devon. Have you tried talking to him to see if he's open to a relationship? If the situation has changed for you, maybe it has for him, too, but you won't know unless you talk."

"I hear you, Wynter. And I thank all of you."

I needed to hear the Gems' advice, especially because over half of them are already in a committed relationship. Everyone else signs off, but Teagan asks me to stay on.

"What's going on?"

"The private investigator I hired for you has news. Is it all right if I give him your contact information so he can meet with you and go over everything?"

"Absolutely." I've been dying to hear what he found out, but have been too afraid to inquire. I didn't want to get my hopes up in case it didn't pan out.

I jot down his name, Neil Beuger, and Teagan says she'll make sure he contacts me right away, then ends the call.

This is really happening. I'll be finding out about my birth father and seeing if we can have some sort of relationship other than the quick hello and goodbye I had with Athena.

I don't fault her. At least she showed up and gave me the

opportunity to ask questions. She even filled out the medi-cal history form about her family, *my biological family*.

Now, all I have to do is wait.

"Are you nervous about seeing your biological father?" Devon asks when he surprises me and stops by my town house later on Friday evening.

"Yes, of course I am, but I'm hoping it goes better than my experience with Athena."

My parents were receptive to my desire to get to know my birth parents. I'm very proud of how they've not only accepted my choices, but championed them. Their accep-tance makes me wonder if I really need to continue down this path, but then again, if I don't, I'll never have the clo-sure I need about my background. No, I must move ahead with the newfound confidence I first found in Aruba and then practiced when reaching out to Athena.

But I am thrilled by Devon's impromptu visit. This is a rare occurrence, especially during the week.

"Where's Kianna?"

"She's over at Chantel's, having a sleepover with Aniya for her birthday."

"That's wonderful," I respond. "And you decided to come here?"

He cocks his head and stares at me. "Yeah, I did. When you texted me about meeting with the private investiga-tor, I was worried about you. Where you able to schedule a meeting?"

I nod. "Monday. He has an office downtown and I'll stop there before lunch."

"If you need to meet me after, I can make myself available."

So he does care about me?

I think about what the Gems said and decide to broach the subject. I just have to figure out how.

"Thank you, that's very kind of you…"

He laughs and pulls me into his lap. "After all these months we've been together, there's no need for you to be so polite, Lyric."

"Speaking of how long we've been together." I turn around on his lap and my bottom makes contact with his crotch. He starts to swell underneath me, but I'm not taking the easy way out by giving in to my bodily urges. Ignoring my desire is hard to do because it's like my body knows his; my nipples pebble in my tank top and I can feel my panties becoming damp.

"Speaking of…" Devon brings me back to the conversation.

"Well, we've been seeing each other often and I was just wondering what it means," I reply nervously, licking my lips.

Confusion crosses his features. "I'm not sure I understand. You know I like you, Lyric. Hell, I can't get enough of you." He reaches to pull me in for a kiss, but I push against his chest.

"Is that all?" I ask. "I know we agreed to keep this a secret because of the school and Kianna, but we have spent a great deal of time in each other's company."

I watch his features harden. I can't breathe waiting for the ball to drop. "Are you saying you want more?"

"Maybe. I at least want to know if there's a possibility for more."

His eyes narrow. "I thought we discussed this months ago. I thought you agreed. I thought you understood."

"I did. I do." The words rush to my lips. "But now I'm checking in again. You're not open to more in the future?"

Devon grabs my hips and sets me away from him. He rises to his feet and turns to face the window looking out at my neighborhood. I can tell I've upset him, but he's trying not to show it. Why can't he talk to me and tell me what's going on?

"Did something happen in the past? With—with your ex-wife? Do you still have feelings for her?" I ask, and nervously keep talking. "I mean, I totally get that, and I don't want to take away from what you had with her."

When he turns back to look at me, his deep-set eyes are haunted. "I'm not still in love with Shiloh. Our marriage wasn't like that."

"Then what was it like?"

"Are you asking me why I'm not diving headfirst into a relationship?"

I don't like his tone, so I just nod.

"Everyone thinks our marriage was some great love story. Because that's what I thought, too. That's how it started… But, well, it wasn't, Lyric. Shiloh was more interested in her dance career than in being a wife, let alone a mother to our baby girl. She couldn't get over what pregnancy did to her body, and maybe she resented Kianna. She loved her work, dance, and she didn't want to make time for anything or anyone else."

I'm floored. His ex-wife was a dancer? Well, that makes sense. Now I understand why Devon was so adamant about Kianna not dancing. And I never told him I was a dancer in Aruba. It had to have come as a shock to him when he learned I owned a dance studio. But more importantly, I can see who Kianna takes after. Somehow she inherited her mother's natural talent.

"So your marriage wasn't a good one?"

He frowns. "No, it wasn't. I confused good sex with love and I won't make that mistake again."

His words are a gut punch. I can't help it; tears prick my eyes. "I see." I uncurl my legs from the sofa and stand. "Well, I'm glad I have a little more of your backstory. Helps explain a lot." I turn and move toward the front door.

"Lyric…"

I open the door and hold it open. "It's been a long day."

He stares at me incredulously. "Are you kicking me out?"

That's exactly what I'm doing. I fold my arms across my chest. I will not be spoken to like that—I'm no one's doormat.

He walks toward me and stops in front of me. "I'm sorry. I shouldn't have said that about us just being about the sex. It was insensitive of me."

I glare at him, unable to speak because I don't want to say anything I'll regret. He stares at me for several more seconds as if I'm going to change my mind. I won't. I need to let everything he's told me settle, then figure out what to do next.

A night apart would serve us well.

"Good night, Lyric," Devon whispers, and I watch his

retreating figure as he heads to his car parked in my drive-way. Then I slam the door and lean back against it.

Damn! I hadn't seen that coming. It feels as if I've been hit by a truck. I know we agreed to be lovers only, but I thought, with how much time we were spending together, that he would be open to a future. Why do I keep reach-ing out to people like Devon and my birth mother who push me away and reject me? I want so badly to belong to someone, but apparently, it won't be Devon.

Devon shared his past with me, but he did so to spite me—to show me we can never have a future. I don't know where to go from here, but it's not as if I can stop loving him.

Because in this moment, with the way I feel after he shut down the possibility of a future together—I know I don't *just* have feelings for Devon.

I'm in love with him.

Devon, however, isn't interested in love or commitment because his ex-wife soured him on relationships. It's been three years and he's still holding on to the anger and hurt from the past. It's why he made all those assumptions and thought the worst of me. I know him keeping me at arm's length is his way of coping with the pain, but right now I'm not sure if he'll ever get over it or even if he wants to try.

Twenty-Eight

Devon

Fuck!

I bang my fists against the steering wheel outside Lyric's home. Why did she have to push my number one taboo subject? I didn't mean to hurt her by insinuating all we are is good sex. I know we're more than the physical, but I also don't know what to do about it.

Slowly, I turn on the engine and pull out of her driveway. I understand Lyric's confusion. Despite my initial proclamation about being secret lovers, we haven't exactly kept to those rules. If Kianna is with me, Lyric spends most nights at my place, in my bed, which is exactly where I want her. And if I'm free, I'm at her place like I am tonight. Except this time, I fumbled, and badly.

My intentions were good. When she expressed her concern over meeting with the investigator and hearing news about her biological father, I felt like she needed me, so I came over. Fortunately, the timing worked and Kianna was at my sister's. I just didn't expect Lyric to ask about what's next in our relationship. She caught me off guard, and I behaved like a total ass. She had every right to kick me out of her town house.

I wanted to be there for her and instead she's probably questioning whether she even wants to be with me.

I've relished the last couple of months we've spent together. Meeting Lyric has been the highlight of my year, and not just mine. I see how happy Kianna is when Lyric's around.

Lyric has a way of bringing out the best in me and Kianna. When I'm with her, I see my cup as half full instead of half empty. Lyric sees life as full of possibilities even though she had a tough break and had to give up her dream of being a ballerina. Instead, she took lemons and made lemonade by opening her own studio. She says she doesn't feel like she belongs and yet she makes everyone feel welcome.

I was curious about Lyric's previous career, and I went online and found some videos of her dancing for the San Francisco Ballet. Many called her the next big thing, and I see why. She was, correction *is,* breathtaking, ethereal and stunning. There are so many more adjectives to describe how Lyric moved across the stage. I was mesmerized.

I couldn't take my eyes off the screen and wanted to see more. I watched every video of Lyric I could find. Since then, I've wondered why I don't see her dancing now, just for herself. I'd love to see her embrace that side of herself again, but maybe she just wants to give back in other ways by teaching her students, by teaching Kianna.

Other parents have shared with me how gifted they think Kianna is and that I should put her in private lessons. I haven't discussed it with my daughter. I guess because I'm afraid of losing my baby girl to a world I don't completely understand, but have learned to appreciate because of Lyric.

Lyric. Lyric. Lyric.

I can't let tonight end like this.

At the light, I make a U-turn and head back to her town house. I don't want her to think I'm treating her like an object or that I'm using her. I care for her. And damn it, I've been trying my best not to, but I do. Shiloh messed me up, did a real number on my head. It's made it hard for me to trust or imagine a romantic future with anyone, but I do care about Lyric. Because of her I feel like the walls I erected around my heart are crumbling. It scares me to feel this way.

I pull into her driveway five minutes later and turn off the engine. Taking a deep breath, I get out of my Mazda and stride to the front door. I ring the doorbell a couple of times and, at first, it appears she's not going to answer, but then the door swings open.

"Devon, what are you doing here?" she asks warily.

"I'm sorry," I say, and step toward her, but she takes a few steps backward, *away* from me. "I'm sorry." I say it again in the hopes this time she hears me.

She rolls her eyes. "I heard you the first time."

"I'm glad because I meant it. I care for you, Lyric."

Her eyes lift to meet mine and my heart constricts at the pain I see lurking in those brown depths. Pain I put there.

I move closer to her and this time, she doesn't move away. She holds her ground.

I reach out and caress her cheek with my palm. "I didn't come back for sex or anything like that. I came back to tell you I'm sorry for hurting you. I don't know if I can offer you what you're looking for."

"But...?" I barely hear the word.

"But I can't give you up," I admit.

"I can't give you up either."

The next thing I know, we're kissing. When I thrust my tongue inside her mouth and our tongues mate, I'm lost, swept up in a fire that consumes us both. I kick the door shut with my foot and seal us in from the world.

"Devon..." Lyric moans.

I slide my lips, firm and demanding, over hers as the kiss becomes more urgent. A gasp escapes her lips and she opens for me. I immediately thrust my tongue deep into her moist warmth, exploring her with a hungry passion. I snake my hand around her waist and pull her close, hip to hip, until her puckered breasts meet my rock-solid body.

I'm aware of nothing but the melting warmth of her. I'm fairly certain I've never wanted anyone this much in my life. I reach down and lift her into my arms, carrying her to her bedroom upstairs.

I waste no time stripping off our clothes so I can sit on the edge of her bed and draw her forward. She straddles my lap and my slumberous gaze fixes on her pert, uplifted breasts. I brush my thumbs across the engorged peaks and she closes her eyes.

Growling, I flick my tongue back and forth across her nipple until she releases a choked cry of pleasure. I like the way she responds to my touch, how open she is with expressing herself. I begin to suck her, laving the stiff peaks with firm, wet lashes of my tongue. Lyric writhes on my lap, making my dick hard underneath her ass.

She feels so good. I want to be inside her, but anticipation is always worth it. I take the other throbbing peak inside my mouth, slowly, making sure she feels all of it, that she's ready for me.

I flip our positions until she's spread out on the bed, her auburn hair fanned around her like an angel. An angel I'm going to feast on. I use my knee, spreading her thighs open, making room for me, and then I dip my head.

Lyric releases a soft moan when I use my mouth and tongue to lick her belly button and the jut of her hip bone. She tenses when I go lower, but I place my palm on her stomach, calming her so she can enjoy the warm heat of my mouth on her wet flesh.

"Devon..." she breathes, eyes on me. "Please."

Her gaze is so hot, I can't wait to consume her and proceed to do just that with possessive laps of my tongue. My breath hitches in my chest.

She has such power over me and she doesn't even know it.

When I feel Lyric's fingers on my head, holding me in place where she wants me, I feast on her. I want to drive her wild until she's shaking and quivering above me. I use all my skills to bring her to the edge just as she does me. One hard lash of my tongue to her tender nub gives me the reaction I seek and her entire body quivers.

Slowly, I ease upward and her palms cup my cheeks. "Please—I need you inside me."

I quickly don protection and slide my palm under the satiny smooth skin of her ass. I rub my dick against her wet opening and then surge inside. Her eyes widen as her body adjusts to mine. When our bodies are locked in an intimate embrace and I'm buried deep inside her, I feel her heartbeat thumping with mine. It's a connection I never knew I wanted, let alone *needed*, but I do. I *need* her.

I slide my hand beneath her bottom and lift her up to meet my hips. She draws my mouth down to hers, kissing me, her nails clawing at my back. I thrust again, deepening my possession of her until she's completely mine. Just when I think it can't get any better, we flip and she's on top. Lyric supports her weight by putting her hands on my chest and begins to ride me. Jesus, the way she undulates her hips makes my eyes roll back in my head. I give up control.

Her breaths start coming in shallow gasps and so do mine. I can't wait to reach that magical place, but we have to do it together. I grab her waist and meet her movements by lifting upward.

She moans.

"Tell me how it feels."

"It feels good...so good. You feel so good, Devon," she whimpers, rolling her hips.

I cup her ass and thrust my dick up inside her. Her eyes widen in surprise.

I notice. "What's wrong?"

"Nothing, it just feels deeper."

I grin. "I'm glad."

When I raise her bottom to hit her sweet spot, a scream shatters the night air. My hands tighten around her hips and I release a shaky breath, drawing back so I can thrust again and increase the pace.

"Devon!" Lyric's back arches and she closes her eyes as a second orgasm strikes her full force. She groans and falls onto my chest in a heap of satisfied bliss.

"Fuck!" I yell as her release causes my own, and we come together in a hot rush of pleasure.

"Devon to earth." Chantel snaps her fingers at me and I realize I've completely missed what she said. She invited me to her place for dinner because according to her all I do is hand Kianna over and leave.

I blink. "Sorry, I zoned out for a minute."

"Is everything okay? Or should I even ask? You have been quite busy lately on the weekends. I wonder if that has something to do with a certain dance teacher?"

My brow furrows. "Pardon?"

"Oh c'mon, Devon. You must know Kianna can't keep a secret. She told me Lyric often comes over to your place for dinner. Does she stay for dessert, too?" Chantel chuckles and I can't help but laugh at her terrible joke.

"I don't kiss and tell."

"But you do kiss." Chantel makes a kissing face.

I roll my eyes at her juvenile behavior. "Yeah, we do."

"See—" she points in my direction "—I knew it. I knew you were creeping."

"If you're suggesting we are keeping this private then the answer would be yes."

"Why? Lyric is a great woman, and from what I hear, she and Kianna get along well."

"What has Kianna said?" I'm curious how my daughter really feels, and will certainly ask her myself, but don't mind getting some insight now.

"She adores Lyric," Chantel responds.

"And? What aren't you saying?"

Chantel shrugs. "Just that Kianna said she could see Lyric as her mother."

My eyes widen in shock. "She said that? I mean, she used those words?"

Chantel nods. "Sure did. If that's not what you wanted, you shouldn't be spending so much time with Lyric."

"That's the problem, Chantel. I thought I knew what I wanted, which was to keep it casual. You know, the occasional hookup, but it's spiraled into something else entirely. And even Lyric questioned me on where this is going."

My sister's lips form an O. "Do tell."

"Last night, Lyric basically wanted to know if our *relationship*, if you can call it that, was going anywhere."

"Good for her. No woman wants to be a booty call."

"That's not what she is, but I can admit I'm unsure of where to go next."

"How about you allow yourself to be happy, Devon?"

A frown mars my features. "I am happy."

"The last couple of months you have been," Chantel replies, "but you're so hard on yourself. You won't allow yourself to go all in with Lyric."

"You saw how my marriage to Shiloh ended. She

wrecked me," I respond. "You know because you had to help pick me up off the floor and care for Kianna."

"Yes, Shiloh hurt you and it was terrible, but it's over. Done. In the past. And bless her soul, Shiloh is gone, but you're still here. Alive and in the present, where Lyric is. You have to live your life and stop looking back."

"That's easy for you to say. You didn't live through what I went through. The pain, the hurt, the confusion. I don't want to go through that again."

"But that's what love is, Devon. Love is about being vulnerable. You have to allow it in order to find love again."

I shake my head. "No, it's not love. We're just kickin' it."

"That's what you say, but your actions speak otherwise." Chantel snorts aloud. "All I'm saying is—don't throw the baby out with the bathwater. Love doesn't have to be all about hurt and pain."

"That's all I know."

Chantel means well but what I endured during my short marriage turned me off the fairy tale of committing myself to another person. The constant arguments, yelling and screaming back and forth. We just weren't meant to be. Always giving and giving without receiving. Not finding that sense of belonging Lyric always talks about.

Not like the belonging I feel with Lyric.

Lyric is one of a kind. She's warm, kind and always willing to lend a helping hand. She's been selfless with my daughter, but it's not just Kianna. I see the way Lyric cares for the other children and teenagers in her classes. Teaching comes naturally to her, even though I saw she was a gifted ballerina. And the fact that she's been able to maintain friendships with the Gems for nearly fifteen years is impressive.

No, *she's* impressive.

Is it enough to make me feel safe enough to take another chance on forever?

Twenty-Nine

Lyric

"Thank you for meeting with me, Mr. Beuger."

I shake the private investigator's hand after arriving at his office on Monday. All weekend I waited for this meeting, but now that it's here, I'm nervous. My heart thuds erratically in my chest and my palms sweat.

"Pleasure to meet you as well," Neil replies. The older gentleman is balding, with salt-and-pepper hair on the sides. He's wearing a polo shirt and khaki pants and looks like a golfer rather than a private investigator. "Please have a seat."

Neil motions to the chair in front of his large glass desk. His office is sleek and modern with a plush leather sofa and bold artwork. I don't know what I expected, but this isn't it. I guess I've watched too many old-school movies about investigators in small, dark offices.

"Were you able to confirm if Jeremy Duncan is my biological father?"

"I have." Neil hands me a manila envelope. "Those are the DNA results."

After some initial fieldwork, Neil made contact with Jeremy Duncan. Jeremy agreed there was a possibility I was his daughter. He remembered Athena coming to him and telling him she was pregnant and he didn't believe her. Neil asked if I would be willing to provide a DNA sample, so I did and here we are.

"So what's next?" I ask.

"You open the test results and if you wish to make contact with Mr. Duncan, I've been authorized to give you his private number."

"It's that easy?" I'm a bit surprised at how smoothly this is going.

"Indeed." When I hesitate to open the envelope, Neil asks, "This is what you wanted? Teagan indicated you wanted to meet your biological father."

Tears well in my eyes and I nod. "I do. I just…after I open this, I can't unsee it. I'll know one way or the other, and I'll have to make some decisions."

"Or you can allow things to remain the status quo. It's your choice."

"Can I take some time with this?" I pat the envelope in my lap.

"Absolutely. In the meantime—" Neil slides a business card across the desk "—that's Mr. Duncan's private line. If you wish to reach him, you can."

I rise to my feet. "Thank you, Mr. Beuger. I appreciate all your hard work and expediency. I didn't expect things to move so quickly."

"Neither did I. You never know in these matters," Neil replies, "but I'm glad it worked out." He extends his hand. "Pleasure doing business with you, Lyric."

"Same." I shake his hand. "Thank you for this." I pat the envelope against my bosom.

I'm leaving Neil's office and not looking in front of me when I hear a feminine voice. "Lyric!"

I glance over and see Teagan's smiling face waiting for me in the lobby of Neil's office building. "Teagan? Wh-what are you doing here?" Teagan is casually dressed in jeans and a leather bomber jacket and not in her usual suit or sheath dress.

"When you told me you were meeting with Neil, I thought you might need some backup," Teagan responds with an open, friendly smile.

"Omigod!" I let out a held-in sigh. "You have no idea how glad I am to see you."

"I know because I know how important this is to you." Teagan pulls me into a hug. I allow her arms to embrace me in a tight squeeze. It's exactly what I need.

When we part, I say, "You're an angel for coming."

"Oh, don't go anointing me for sainthood or anything, but it's what we Gems do. We stand by each other." She circles her arm through mine. "What do you say we get some lunch?"

"Sounds marvelous."

★ ★ ★

Twenty minutes later, we're seated at my favorite Mexican lunch spot. Teagan orders us some margaritas. "I think you could use some libation."

"I think I could, too."

The waiter comes over and we order some chips, guacamole and fajitas to accompany our drinks. Once he's gone, we start catching up.

"When did you get here?" I ask.

"This morning. A red-eye to make sure I was here in enough time. Egypt was going to come, too, because she's the closest, but her sous-chef Quentin called out sick last night and she had to stay back at Flame."

"I appreciate you guys were even thinking about me."

"We might be far away from each other," Teagan responds, "but we will never give up on you."

Her fierce words touch a place in my soul. "You know I feel the same way and will be there for you if you need me."

"Of course, but you know me, Lyric," Teagan says. "I'm impenetrable. Not many people can get past my defenses."

"They should, because they are missing out on a wonderfully kind and giving human being."

"You're too soft, Lyric." Teagan smiles back at me, but I can tell my words have hit their mark because her dark brown eyes soften. "I worry about you. Even when we were in school, you were so slender and fragile. I felt like I had to look out for you like a big sister."

"You don't need to. I can take care of myself. Besides, missy, we're the same age."

Teagan huffs out a laugh. "Are we? I feel old beyond my years. I was proud to see you went all out in Aruba. But what's going on with you and Devon?"

I let out a loud chuckle. "Omigod. I've totally missed you." Teagan is much like Egypt; they have no filter. They confidently say whatever comes to their minds while I'm more cautious.

The waiter returns with our margaritas and we toast, but then Teagan gives me the eagle eye. "Don't think you're going to avoid the subject at hand. Devon?" She gives me a gentle nudge.

"We're doing fine." I take a sip of the drink, slather a chip with guacamole and munch on it. "I took Wynter's advice and asked him about a relationship."

"And?" One of her brows rises.

"He wasn't a fan. Apparently, his marriage was terrible. His ex was only interested in being a dancer and not a wife, or a mother to Kianna, which I totally can't understand because that little girl is adorable."

"You've fallen in love with them, haven't you?"

"Them?"

"Devon and Kianna. The way you talk about Devon's daughter, I can see how much you care for her."

"I do. She's a special little girl."

"And her Daddy?"

"Is hot and sexy. Damn it, Teagan! I want them both."

Teagan nods. "And does he want you?"

"Physically? Yes. Emotionally? I know he cares for me. He knew I was nervous about meeting my biological father and he came over to comfort me. I'm just not sure if he's ready for the *more* portion."

"Love?"

I sigh and nod. "And that's scary because I think I'm already there."

"Lyric…"

"I don't really want to talk about it, okay? I have enough on my plate." I glance down at the manila envelope sticking out of my purse.

"Are you ready to open it?" Teagan inquires. "I'm here either way."

"Yes, I want to, and I'm glad you're here." I reach for the envelope and slide my finger underneath the flap, ripping it open. Slowly, I pull out one sheet of paper labeled "DNA results."

I glance over it and see that with 97 percent chance of accuracy, Jeremy Duncan is my biological father. I swallow the lump in throat and suck in deep mouthfuls of air.

"Well?" Teagan's voice is quiet and respectful.

I glance up with tears shimmering in my eyes. "He's my father."

Teagan reaches across the table and grasps my hand. "Well, now you know, no more uncertainty."

I nod. "I just have to get up the courage to call him."

"There's no time like the present," Teagan replies.

I stare at her with large eyes. "Teagan!"

"You've already procrastinated about this for months. You've ripped off the Band-Aid, go all the way."

I know she's right. I've known who he is since meeting Athena, but I was afraid to go there. Afraid of being rejected again. I want so much to have a family of my own and to belong. I reach inside my purse and pull out the business card Neil gave me.

Without wasting time to think about what comes next, I tap in the digits. My biological father answers on the second ring.

"Jeremy Duncan speaking." His voice is smooth and deep like Barry White.

"Mr. Duncan. My name is Lyric Taylor, and I'm your daughter."

My call with Jeremy is short but goes as well as can be expected. He isn't stunned by my declaration. Instead, he's excited to meet me. We make plans for when he returns, because he's out of town with a recording artist for the next couple of weeks. It's a bit anticlimactic, but I don't have any other choice except to wait.

Teagan stays with me the entire time and when I hang up, I want to throw up.

"Well?" she asks, staring at me. "It went good?"

"Yes, I—I can't believe I did it," I reply, holding my stomach as my belly flip-flops. "Thank you for pushing me."

"You're welcome." Teagan gives a little shrug. "Do you need me to stay longer? My flight is later this afternoon."

"Absolutely not. Jeremy doesn't get back for a couple of weeks. I'll be fine until then. Besides, you have a successful brokerage business to run."

"I do, but that's why I have good people who can handle things in my absence."

"And I get it, but no, I can handle this on my own," I reply. "You got me this far. I've got the rest."

"Excellent, because our food is here and I'm starved. Food in first class is not what it used to be."

We finish up our lunches. Afterward I drive Teagan to my studio so she can see what I've done with the place since the grand opening.

"I'm so proud of you, Lyric." Teagan's heels click on the hardwood floors of the studio as she walks around. "Not everyone gets to live out two of their life's dreams, but you have. I think we Gems always thought you were the quiet one, but it's the quiet determination that's put you here." She motions around the room.

"It would be a mistake to underestimate me. I might be small, but I'm mighty."

A broad smile crosses Teagan's beautiful features. "Yes, you are."

We spend some time going over my recordkeeping, and after Teagan is dutifully impressed and has given me a bit of advice, because she can't seem to help herself, we head to the airport so she can make her flight. When I pull up to the terminal, I jump out of the car and give her a big hug.

"Thank you. You didn't have to come today to be here for me, but you did. I'll never forget it. Love you, girl."

After we part, she gives me a kiss on the cheek. "Love you, too." And with a wave, she walks inside.

I'm getting back into the car when my phone rings and my car display reads "Devon."

"Babe, I'm so sorry," Devon says. "I got overwhelmed at work. How did it go today? Did you get the results?"

Did he just call me babe?

"Um, it went really well," I respond and fill him in on the details of meeting the private investigator and Teagan's surprise visit.

"Your Gems are the best!" Devon says. "I'm so sorry I didn't get a chance to meet her."

I'm just about to say "You will," but will he? Will we be together long enough for him to meet the special women in my life?

"Me, too," I say instead. "Another time."

Although Devon didn't nix the idea of a relationship between us entirely, neither is he telling me how he wants to spend more time with me. I'm in such a pickle. As Teagan said, I'm in love with him and Kianna. I can see them as my family, but I also can't have that dream with them if Devon doesn't feel the same way.

Right now, I need to put it aside. Once I get through the first meeting with my biological father, then there will be a reckoning coming for me and Devon.

Thirty

Lyric

The next couple of weeks go by in a blur. I'm glad the studio is busy with new students and recital rehearsals for existing students because it keeps me from worrying about how my meeting with Jeremy will go. Since one of my two instructors is visiting a sick family member and doesn't know how long she'll be out, I've been covering the majority of the academy's classes.

I've had to cancel my plans with Devon the last couple of weekends. Usually my schedule is flexible and I can carve out time to see him, but between tap, ballet and jazz classes, I'm worn out every night. All I can do is crawl up the stairs of my town house, have a hot shower and go straight to bed.

Saturday arrives before I can blink, and Devon brings Kianna to class. He gives me a wave because they arrived late and class is about to start. I've been teaching Kianna's level all the classic ballet moves from first position to fifth position. The girls are remembering the relevé, tendu and pliés while learning chassé, arabesque, rond de jambe, sauté, tombé pas de bourrée, coupé, passé, glissade and the pirouette.

That's the hardest move to learn, but all the young girls in the class have seen it on television or in the movies. It's taking a lot of practice, along with a lot of patience on my part, to help them master it. I'm helping them put it all together into a dance for their recital, but it'll be a marathon, not a sprint.

When the class ends, I'm finally able to speak with Devon.

"Hey, stranger," he says after Kianna's class ends and I'm walking toward my office.

"Hello, Mr. Masters. Good to see you," I reply since several parents are lingering in the hall. "Can I speak with you in my office for a moment?"

"Sure thing," Devon replies. "Kianna, I'll be right back."

He follows me into my office and once there he closes the door and pulls me toward him. His mouth brushes over mine in a slow, gentle caress that leaves me clamoring for more.

Devon lifts his head a fraction and stares into my eyes. "I've missed you."

"I'm sorry. It's been crazy busy here."

He nods and then lowers his head once more to capture my lips in a drugging kiss that leaves me boneless against the door. When his tongue probes the line of my lips, I greedily open my mouth and gasp as he deepens our kiss. I shiver with excitement when his fingers slide over my leotard and close around my breasts.

I moan and tip my head back, because his mouth has left mine and is now grazing a path down my neck to *my spot*.

"Devon, we can't." I push him away. If he reaches that spot, there's no going back. I'll let him take me up against this door with children and parents in the hall.

His eyes glitter like twin orbs of fire. "I know, I know, but I wanted to give you a taste of what's to come later."

"You have," I respond, taking a sharp breath. "But I have to get back out there. I have another class."

"I'll see you later?" he asks, hopefully.

"That's the goal."

"Are you sure about that?" His eyes narrow, and it's clear he doesn't like my answer.

I don't take the bait, and he steps aside, allowing me to precede him into the corridor. Surely he's not angry because I'm busy at the studio and not able to find time for us?

I remember him mentioning that Shiloh didn't have time for him, that she was consumed by her career, but that's not me. I know Devon was hurt by her disinterest, but his tendency to jump to conclusions is so aggravating. It's not as if my schedule is always this busy. I'm usually available, and the few times I'm not, he's copping an attitude?

This is my busy season. I need to know I have his support and that he won't fly off the deep end. I don't need this extra emotional labor when I'm navigating a new business and a new career as a teacher.

I don't have time to discuss it, though, so I plaster a smile on my face and go into my next session. But the thought has taken root and I can't seem to find my focus. I power through the remaining few classes until 4:00 p.m. when I teach my last class. It takes another couple of hours before I'm fully finished with all my administrative work and have updated my social media with the clips from today's classes. I wish I had someone to handle this portion of the work, but I signed up to be my own boss. So I have to take the good with the bad.

I close up the studio and head home. When I arrive, Devon is already parked in front of the town house. Well, that was presumptuous of him. Even though we'd talked about the possibility of meeting tonight, we'd never confirmed. How did he know I wasn't bringing someone else home or hadn't planned on a quiet evening after a stressful week? Not that I would have the time or even want anyone else.

Devon is the only man I've been with or talked to since Aruba, but that isn't the point. Devon hasn't made it clear whether he's willing to entertain being in a relationship with me even though I mentioned this weeks ago. I know I wanted to wait until after my meeting with Jeremy to confront him, but his behavior earlier has me reconsidering.

Slowly, I exit my vehicle and he does the same, meeting me at my door. He takes my bags from my hands, which hold my uniforms in need of washing, some microwave bowls from the lunch I brought with me and paperwork I need to review.

"Thanks," I say, and unlock the front door.

Devon follows me inside to the kitchen, plops the bags on the counter and comes over to me. "Everything okay?"

"Why wouldn't it be?" My voice is tight and strained.

"I don't know, you seem like you're in a mood," Devon replies. "Did I do something wrong?"

I shake my head. "No, I'm just tired."

"Too tired to give me a proper hello?" he asks with a grin.

I walk over to him and lift my head to accept his kiss. It's hard to hold on to anger when his lips are gentle and tender and so beguilingly sweet. He easily coaxes a response from me. My breasts ache and that familiar sensation makes a pit in my stomach, the sensation that forms whenever Devon is near.

Devon breaks the kiss and stares down at me. His eyes glitter with passion.

"Devon, I'm tired," I state. As much as I love his kisses, his behavior from earlier today is still sticking in my craw. I suppose it's been a long couple of weeks, between work, the situation with my biological father and being emotionally vulnerable with Devon without getting the commitment I need.

"I expected you would be so I ordered in," he responds. "The food should be here any minute. I ordered your favorite Thai."

I can't help but smile at his thoughtfulness. He does things like this, which make me think he cares, but then he's a contradiction when he refuses to state that he wants to be with me long-term. He knows how much I want to belong and have a family of my own, yet he can't agree that a future together is a possibility.

"There's definitely something wrong," Devon says, staring at me when I don't respond. "Do you want to tell me what's bothering you? Are you worried about your father's return next week?"

I shake my head. "No, it's not that."

"Then what is it?" Devon presses. "Is it me?"

When I'm silent, he stares back at me incredulously. "What have I done that's upset you?"

I exhale audibly. "It's what you haven't done, Devon, that's the problem."

His eyes narrow. "Meaning?"

I toss my hands up in the air. "It's been months, and I guess I've reached my breaking point. I need answers. One moment, you want me in your life, spending time with you and Kianna. On the next breath, you tell me you don't want love or commitment or any sort of relationship, that we should stay a secret. Then you're back to doing thoughtful things for me, like ordering Thai food after a long week and saying you can't give me up. Which is it?"

"For Christ's sake, Lyric." Devon runs his hands through his hair. "I'm trying here, okay? You know how hard this is for me, that I've been building trust with you after being hurt in the past with Shiloh."

"Yes, I know that, Devon, I do. And I've given you grace, but you also have to give me a reason to stay in the fight. I need hope that one day we can have a future together."

"That's what I've been doing. I've been trying to open up to you slowly. Do you have any idea how hard this is for me, especially with all the similarities between this situation and the past? You're a dancer, just like my ex-wife, and now you're working just as hard as she did. I've barely seen you in weeks."

"Two weeks!" I yell. I'm so frustrated with Devon's hot and cold behavior. It's too much. This is not how I want to live my life. "I'm busy for two weeks, and you're comparing me to your dead ex?"

"It's about so much more than the work," Devon responds, shaking his head and pacing. "I never came first with Shiloh. Kianna and I were always an afterthought. So is it hard for me seeing you work like this? Yes, because it me brings me back to the past and how I felt back then. Like I wasn't good enough, like dance would always come before me."

"That's not fair, Devon." I hate that tears sting my eyes at his harsh words. "I have never done that. Since I've met you, I have put your needs, Kianna's needs, above my own, but what about what I want?"

His eyes search mine. "What do you want, Lyric?"

"I want you," I cry. "I want you to want me as much as I want you. I want you to love me and say you'll be with me not just for now, but for the long-term because you see a future for us."

Devon lowers his head. "Why do you have to have everything right now, Lyric? Why can't you just let things happen naturally and we can see where this goes?"

"Because..." I almost say the words, but Devon isn't ready to hear them. He's fighting me at every turn. Does he feel something for me?

"Because what?" Devon presses.

"Does it matter?" I reply. "Your guard is up. It will always be up because you're afraid of getting hurt again, but I didn't hurt you, Devon. I shouldn't be punished for how Shiloh treated you. I should have a clean slate. I deserve that."

Devon sighs and lowers his head. I watch him rub the back of his neck. When he finally looks at me, there's regret in his eyes—exactly what I didn't want to see.

Don't do it.

Please don't do it.

"I think it's best if we take some time apart, Lyric," Devon responds. "We've been together for nearly three months now. Things have moved quickly. Perhaps too quickly. Some time apart would give us perspective and allow us to figure out what it is that we want."

I know what I want. It's you.

But I remain silent. I'm certainly not about to beg him to stay with me. Yet at the same time, I'm crushed. I love him. I love him more than I knew I was capable of loving another human being.

I love Kianna, too. I've enjoyed being in her life. I don't want to lose that.

"What about Kianna?" She shouldn't have to suffer or stop her ballet, which she loves so much.

"She can still come to class. I can have my sister Chantel drop her off or I'll figure something out."

So he doesn't want to see me at all? The pain is innumerable, but I take it. I think about all the physical pain I endured as a dancer and channel that energy as Devon breaks my heart.

I nod. "Okay."

Devon stares me for a long moment, but I look away. I

can't meet his eyes. Not now. I'm afraid of what he might see if he peers at me too closely. When I glance up again, he's walking toward the door.

The doorbell rings.

Devon answers and I watch him pay the delivery driver and take the plastic bags of food. He brings them over to the kitchen where I'm still standing. I can't move. I'm frozen.

"Keep the food," he says. "With your busy schedule, you need to eat." He starts for the door, and I wonder if that's it.

Is that really how this ends?

But then Devon turns one more time. "I'm sorry, Lyric. You're right, you deserve so much better. I'm sorry I can't be the man you need me to be."

Then he quietly walks out of my town house and closes the door. Once he's left my driveway, I fall to the kitchen floor and let out a sob.

Thirty-One

Devon

Why did she have to push me to say things that hurt her?

I came to her place with the best intentions—to be helpful after she'd had a difficult couple of weeks. Was I upset because her behavior reminded me of Shiloh? Yes. It made me think of all the missed dinners, parties and events Shiloh could never make because her job came first.

Before me.

Before Kianna.

I think it's because Shiloh never really wanted to have children to begin with. She went along with it because I was so happy and so excited to be a father. I always wanted a family of my own because I hadn't grown up in one. I was the ultimate latchkey kid coming home from school and making myself a snack until my mother got in from work.

Learning Shiloh and I were going to have a child made

me long for that traditional family with a mother and a father. I wanted that for Kianna, but Shiloh had other dreams. Dreams that didn't include me, and once Kianna was born, the cracks in our relationship became more evident. We weren't going to last. We wanted different things out of life. And then she passed away before we could figure it out. I had to accept that, but it wasn't easy giving up on my dreams of family either.

And now I see similarities with Lyric.

Her work ethic is commendable. She's the sole owner of LT Dance Academy, and I understand everything falls on her shoulders. So I pushed down my reservations about being with her and persevered. We could get through this.

Or that's what I thought.

But she wants more than I'm capable of. I told her all I could offer was an affair, and Lyric said she understood. She told me her reputation was important, that she didn't want it damaged by parents knowing we were lovers. I was hoping that was enough.

My marriage broke me, made me cold, bitter—but being with Lyric was like coming out of a long, hard winter into the bright sunshine of spring. Her incandescence ignites a light in the darkness of my soul in a way I didn't think was possible after Shiloh. The thought of losing her...

But she wants a relationship, and that brings a host of complications. I'm not sure I can give her what she wants, what she needs. I've lived too long without trust, openness and vulnerability. I don't need them.

Some time and space apart is what we need. Distance

will help me navigate how to handle this situation we find ourselves in, figure out what to do next.

It won't be easy because Kianna goes to Lyric's dance studio and not only loves it, but she also adores Lyric. And as much as I'm not a fan of ballet, I have learned more about it than I once knew. I would never deny Kianna the opportunity to be taught by someone of Lyric's caliber. Yet at the same time, I don't know how I'll watch Lyric week after week and not want to do whatever it takes to be the man she needs me to be.

"Why isn't Lyric coming over anymore?" Kianna asks me two weeks later, after I pick her up from LT Dance Academy and we're back home on the sofa. She's got on the pink glittery tutu dress Lyric bought her, which happens to be one of her favorites.

When I came into the academy earlier with Kianna, I found Lyric on the floor in a ballerina split position with her legs straight out and toes pointed. She looked incredibly sexy. I know how flexible she can be and my groin twitched. As if she could feel me, Lyric glanced up from her exercise, and our eyes locked. She held my gaze, and I was unable to look away until Kianna tugged my hand.

So while Kianna was in class I went to my car to sulk and hide. I can't watch Lyric right now. It's too much. Too soon. I miss her, and apparently so does Kianna.

"Miss Lyric is very busy now, honey," I respond to Kianna's question. "Her academy has a lot of new students."

"She's never been too busy for me," Kianna replies, and

her lower lip forms into a pout. "Why doesn't she want to spend time with us? Does she not like us anymore?"

"Of course she likes us." I pull Kianna into my lap. "Lyric adores you as much as I do."

Kianna frowns, "You're supposed to love me, you're my dad. But Lyric is my friend."

"And she still is," I respond. "That hasn't changed." And I'll have to ensure it doesn't. Even though Lyric and I aren't together right now, I don't want Kianna to suffer or feel less than absolutely loved.

Loved.

That's the problem.

Love is an emotion I've steered clear of, other than the fatherly love I have for Kianna. Romantic love again? I've not allowed for that possibility because I don't want to risk feeling the way I felt after my marriage ended so horribly. I hated how everything I believed when I married Shiloh got ripped away. All my hopes and dreams about love and marriage, partnership and family, blew up in my face. So I hardened my heart, but damn it if Lyric doesn't have me questioning all my decisions around relationships.

All week long I've thought about her and wondered what she was doing, hoping she would see reason so we could be together. I miss our intimacy, and not just the incredible physical harmony of us joining our bodies.

I shudder. My feelings for Lyric aren't like anything I've felt before. They make me want to believe there could be a future, a happy ending. And that makes me nervous.

"Can I call Miss Lyric?" Kianna asks.

"Of course you can." I dig into my pocket and produce

my phone. My hands tremble as I swipe to find Lyric's name. My heart pounds when I press the call button and put it on speaker.

Lyric answers with a tentative, "Hello?"

I immediately hand the phone over to Kianna, who excitedly grabs it out my hand. "Hi, Miss Lyric. It's Kianna."

"Oh, Kianna." I can hear the disappointment in her voice. Was she expecting it to be me? What if had been? Would we have gotten back to where we once were? Doubtful. "How are you, sweetheart?"

"I'm good. I was just wondering if you might come over tonight?" Kianna asks.

I shake my head furiously at Kianna to indicate that isn't a good idea, but she's already jumping off my lap and walking away from me with my phone.

"I'm sorry, but I have other plans tonight," Lyric responds, "but I can pick you up tomorrow and we can go have breakfast, just you and me. How does that sound?"

"What about Daddy?" Kianna asks.

Jumping up from the sofa, I stride over to where my daughter is curled up in the recliner. "It's okay, Kianna. You and Miss Lyric go and have some fun girl time."

"See?" I hear the smile in Lyric's voice. "It's settled. I'll swing by and pick you up around ten o'clock."

"Awesome! See you tomorrow," Kianna says, and she disconnects the phone. I want to thank Lyric for still being there for my daughter, but the call has already ended.

Is this how it's going to be? Lyric having a relationship with my daughter while she and I are on the outs? I want to pick up the phone and tell her to make it like it was, but only *I* can change that. Lyric asked me if there was a chance *we* could be more. My heart wants me to admit we could be, but my head reminds me of the pain I endured during my marriage.

I listen to my head and don't call her back.

Thirty-Two

Lyric

Kianna excitedly rambles on about her week and what I've missed since we last hung out together. She talks about her first-grade teacher and the new best friend she made in class. We talk about the recital and how happy she is to have a solo if only for a few minutes. She's been practicing her pirouettes, and I know she's going to do great. We talk about everything except the elephant in the room.

Her father.

When I arrived to pick her up, Devon opened the door looking as sexy as ever in faded denim jeans and a graphic T-shirt. I wanted him to pull me into his arms and tell me he'd made a mistake, but instead, he merely called out for Kianna, who came running up behind him and threw herself at me.

"I missed you," she said, curling her arms around my neck.

I glanced up at her father and said, "I missed you, too." And gave Kianna a tight squeeze before rising to my feet. "Are you ready for some chocolate chip pancakes with maple syrup?"

"Yes!" Kianna clapped.

"All right then." I glanced over in Devon's direction, but he was silent throughout our interaction. It hurt to feel his cold dismissal of everything we shared. I guess I should be happy he's not ending my relationship with Kianna like he ended ours.

But did we ever really have one?

Devon went to great pains to make sure I knew he could only offer me sex and companionship, nothing more. Did I go into this affair with my eyes wide-open? Yes. Except he unwittingly gave me more than sex. His kindness, tenderness, compassion, thoughtfulness made me believe he felt more for me than just the physical.

With Devon, I've been freer and more liberated sexually than I have with any other man in my life. During our time together in Aruba and after, I garnered a newfound confidence in myself. It allowed me to take risks in the bedroom, and in life, like finally meeting my biological parents.

But he's still holding on to the past.

I've worked through so many issues surrounding my past. And he's right. There's no future for us if he can't do the same.

Though he hasn't exactly called it off. Instead he took the coward's way out by saying we need time and space. Does that mean he might change his mind and let me into his heart?

Why am I doing this to myself?

He doesn't want me. If he did, he wouldn't have let me walk out of his life.

Now I focus my attention on Kianna. I still have her in my life, even if I don't have her father. She brings me such joy, but I don't know how much longer I'll have her since Devon and I are not together. So I'll make the most of every moment.

Once we're at the breakfast shop and seated in a booth, I look over the menu. "Do you want sausage or bacon with your pancakes?" I inquire, even though I already know the answer.

"Sausage, please," she responds, and then uses the crayons the waitress gave her to color.

I order Kianna a plate of sausage, eggs and pancakes while I opt for the Greek omelet with spinach and feta.

"Ugh. Spinach in your eggs?" Kianna makes a face.

"Vegetables are good for you."

"If you say so." Kianna returns to her coloring book and then casually drops the question. "Are you mad at Daddy or something?"

I frown. Did she pick up on the anxiety between us earlier? "No, not at all."

She glances up at me through her thick lashes. She looks so much like Devon, with his deeply set brown eyes, round nose and warm nutty brown complexion. "You didn't hug him like you usually do."

She noticed that?

"I was just so excited to see you, Kianna."

She nods her head. "I think he misses you, too. You're

the first friend Daddy has had over to the house other than Auntie Chantel. And he's been sad for weeks."

"Is that right?"

Kianna nods and glances up at me. "I think he gets lonely. He needs a friend like you to keep him company."

I laugh at Kianna's keen observation. I'd been doing a lot more than being his companion. There's no place in the house where we haven't made love.

"That's good to know," I reply. "I'll do my best."

When she glances up again, her eyes are misty with tears. "You promise?"

I reach across the table for her little hand. "I promise."

She nods. "Because my mommy left and never came back. She went to heaven, you know."

"Yes, I heard. Do you miss her, too?"

Kianna shakes her head. "No. Not like I miss you. She didn't come around much before she went to heaven. But you're different."

Tears burn my eyes at Kianna's honesty—out of the mouths of babes. I'm glad I'm different from Shiloh. If a six-year-old can see it, surely Devon can see I'm not his ex-wife? We could have such a great life, if only...

But I can't base my life on "if onlys." If he can't see how good we can be together, I have to move on without him.

The day has arrived to meet my biological father. After all the angst and anxiety of the last few months, it feels anticlimactic to finally have this meeting. I've been so upset about Devon and my ending things, I haven't had much time to worry about how today might go.

We're meeting in the park. Some place neutral where we don't have to worry about people listening in. Although he's not famous like his clients, folks in Memphis know Jeremy Duncan. I was going to suggest my town house, but if today goes off the rails, I wanted to be able to go home to my safe haven.

I've dressed in a simple floral maxi dress with a belt around the middle and my jean jacket. I love Memphis in the cool of spring. I teamed the outfit with a pair of sandals and gold hoop earrings. Needing a caffeine fix, I stopped by Starbucks along the way for a java chip Frappuccino. I need a treat for whatever awaits me.

After parking my Camry, I walk to our designated meeting spot. My stomach is tied up in knots and I can hear my heart thudding loudly in my chest. I remind myself I already have wonderful parents. Mama's and Daddy's faces flood my mind. No matter what happens I have their love and support.

As I approach, I notice a tall gentleman rise from a bench several feet away. He has to be at least six feet and has skin the color of café au lait, same as me. He's wearing a brown button-down shirt, beige slacks and Gucci loafers. I stop walking mid-stride. My first inclination is to retreat and save myself from whatever disappointment is coming my way.

He smiles as I get closer, and I notice he has hazel eyes. "Lyric?"

I nod because my throat has completely closed up; I can't speak. Tears threaten as I come face-to-face with my biological father. Staring back at me is a face similar to my own, from the shape of his mouth to his round nose.

Jeremy comes toward me, and I want to back away but find I'm frozen in place. He wraps his arms around me, and I gulp hard, unable to accept he's embracing me. Tears slip down my cheeks.

Jeremy rubs my back, hugging me tightly as if he never wants to let me go. "It's okay, Lyric. I'm just as emotional as you are."

I pull myself away and stare back at him.

Tears stain his cheeks.

"Can we sit down?"

I don't answer, but follow him to the park bench where we sit side by side. The impact of this moment isn't lost on either of us. We're both silent for a few minutes, gathering our thoughts and emotions.

After a moment, Jeremy turns to me. "I'm sorry. I'm sorry I haven't been in your life. Athena tried to tell me she was pregnant, but I was a young knucklehead back then and thought myself a player. I didn't want to accept what I knew, which was that I was the only boy she'd been with. Athena was a good churchgoing girl and I ruined her like I ruined so many girls."

I nod. What else am I supposed to do with that confession? He ruined other girls? So there's the possibility I have siblings?

"As far as I know, you're my only offspring." Jeremy responds to my unspoken question with a laugh. "If I have any other children they haven't come forward."

I finally find my voice. "Thank you for meeting with me. I wasn't sure you would want to."

A frown mars his features. "Why wouldn't I? It's not your

fault I abandoned Athena in her time of need, leaving her no choice but to put you up for adoption. How are your adoptive parents? Are they good people?"

His question brings a smile to my face. "The Taylors are the best parents I could ever have. I've always felt loved and protected."

His body sways back and forth and a tear slides down his round cheek. "I'm glad. In the music industry, I've heard horror stories of kids being caught in the system and abused. I was hoping that didn't happen to you, to my daughter."

His words make me inhale sharply.

My daughter.

Athena never called me that. She acknowledged she gave birth to me, but nothing more.

"What do you want us to be?" I ask.

"That's entirely up to you," Jeremy replies. "I've literally dropped into your life like some sort of bomb, and I don't want to detonate it or ruin your relationship with your family in any way. But if you might want to hang out from time to time and get to know me, I wouldn't mind." He sighs and then corrects. "I would like that very much."

I stare at him in confusion and bewilderment. I never expected to have such a greeting or to be accepted without question and with open arms. "I—I…"

He pats my knee. "You don't have to decide now, Lyric. I'm just happy you were willing to meet me. You must be so angry at me and Athena for not being there for you."

I shake my head. "Maybe if I'd grown up differently, with parents who didn't love me, maybe I might feel that way, but I don't. I just wanted to know where I came from." Tears blind my eyes and choke my voice. It takes me a few moments to continue. "I-I wanted to know who I look like, and today I got my answer."

"You look like me," Jeremy finishes.

I nod.

"Is there anything you want to know?" he inquires.

"Yeah." I laugh wryly. "Everything. We have thirty years to make up for."

He smiles back at me warmly. "Yes, we do." He inclines his head to my drink. "I know you're drinking a coffee, but what do you say to some lunch? I'm starved, and we have a lot of catching up."

"I would like that very much."

He stands to his feet and holds out his hand to help me up.

This meeting did not go as I thought it would. It went better, and I'm so excited to learn more about my biological father. I'll have to figure out what place he'll have in my life, if he'll be a part of my family, but for now I'm soaking up the knowledge that he wants to get to know me.

It's more than I expected after the inauspicious meeting with Athena, but I'm putting that in the past and facing the future. I may not have Devon in my life, but I have my parents, my biological father and the Gems. I belong to an extraordinary family, some new and some old, who love and support me. There's nothing but good things ahead.

Thirty-Three

Devon

"What do you think, Daddy?"

Kianna twirls around in a brand-new red tutu dress I bought for her recital later today. She and my niece Aniya have been rehearsing for weeks at Lyric's dance studio.

"I think you look amazing," I respond.

"So do I," Chantel replies. "You both look amazing. Miss Lyric is going to be so proud of both of you."

Kianna beams at the praise. "I hope so. I've been practicing so hard."

"Me too," Aniya says, and executes a ballet move I've seen Kianna do a ton of times, but don't recall the name.

I move away and head to the kitchen for a beer. I pull one out of the fridge and lean against the counter, watching the girls.

Today is going to be hard. I'll have to see Lyric, watch

her from afar, but not touch her. I've stuck by my decision to keep my distance, to evaluate if our affair was working for both of us. If I'm honest, I miss her. I wonder how she's doing. Her meeting with her father was this week, and I want to ask how it went, but do I have a right to? I'm the one who asked for time and space.

"And why do you look like you've lost your puppy dog?" Chantel asks, joining me in the kitchen away from young listening ears.

I chuckle. "I don't have a dog."

Chantel rolls her eyes. "You know what I mean. You look down in the dumps and I suspect I know why."

Turning, I give her a hard glare. "And what is it that you *think* you know?"

"Kianna told me Ms. Lyric hasn't come by to visit you in weeks *and* you used to always like taking the girls to class, but suddenly you're busy and unable to take them on the weekends."

"What's that got to do with anything?"

"I think you've been avoiding going to the studio because you guys broke up. And why may I ask? Lyric is amazing. You're not going to find another woman who is as into you or who loves your daughter as much."

I tip my beer back and take a swig. "I don't need you to remind me of that fact."

"Maybe you do. Because you're messing up, Devon. You got it right this time. I know things didn't work out with your first marriage, but you've got a good thing going with Lyric. Don't let your fears get in the way of you having the love and happiness you so richly deserve."

"Did anyone ever tell you you can be rather pushy?"

"My husband Chris does all the time," Chantel replies. I laugh out loud. My sister definitely wears the pants in *her* marriage. "But don't go changing the subject. You have to get her back."

I shake my head. "It's been weeks, Chantel, and Lyric hasn't come back to me. She came by to pick up Kianna last week and took her out for breakfast and barely gave me a glance."

"Why should she? You should be fighting for her because you're probably the reason you're in this predicament to begin with."

My brow furrows. "You're my sister, you're supposed to be on my side."

"I am. But I also have to point out when you're screwing up. You might be older but that doesn't mean you can't learn from me. In case you hadn't noticed, I've been happily married for over a decade now."

"I do know. And I've been envious of what you and Chris share because I wanted that once, and when it went sideways, I didn't know how to handle it, still don't. I certainly didn't expect to be a single father."

"But you did it. You carved out a life for you and Kianna. Look how happy she is. She's a beautiful, well-adjusted little girl, and that's all because of you."

I give her a sideways glance. "Don't lay it on so thick."

She chuckles. "Is it working? Are you going to try to fix what's broken?"

"I don't know if I can."

And I'm almost afraid to try. I don't think I could stand

it if Lyric turned her back on me for good. I know I asked for distance, but I miss her zest for life, her passion—for me, her friends and her family, which Kianna and I would like to be a part of.

Chantel squeezes my arm. "You can do this, Devon. Do it for yourself and for that little girl." She inclines her head toward Kianna, who is dancing and prancing around with Aniya. "Because she loves Lyric and I think you do, too. You've just been too afraid to admit it."

I'm stunned at my sister's words, and only faintly hear Chantel tell me she'll take the girls early to the recital. She leaves me alone with my thoughts.

Do I love Lyric?

The instant the question comes to my mind, I freeze, unable to breathe.

Lyric, her face alight with passion as she kisses me with a sensuality I've never known.

Lyric, touching me as if I'm precious and belong to her.

Lyric, who is so strong, who fought my issues about dancing so my talented little girl can chase her dream.

Lyric, who has always been open, honest and generous to me and my daughter and all she asks for in return is to belong.

Lyric, who loves my daughter.

Is it possible she could love me, too?

I think about how hurt she was when I asked for distance, and I know the answer.

How could I have been so blind? She's who I need. Who fate sent into my life with a hotel mix-up.

Closing my eyes, I face the truth. Ever since I met Lyric,

I've been wrapped up in her, been so mad *at her* and *about her*. She slammed herself past all my protective layers and unearthed an emotion I didn't think I could feel again.

Love.

I am in love with her.

I think I have been since Aruba, but I was too afraid to admit it to myself for fear of getting hurt, for fear of not being wanted or loved again. But I shouldn't be scared of loving Lyric. I should be embracing it, embracing her.

I made a terrible mistake in letting her go.

I have to make it right.

Rushing out of the room, I grab my car keys off the console and head toward the door to get ready for the performance of my life.

To convince Lyric to take me back.

Thirty-Four

Lyric

The girls are nervous as they rehearse in the small green-room.

I rented out a neighborhood theater so my students could have the experience of dancing in front of a live audience for the spring recital. For some of my older clients, if this is truly a passion they want to pursue, they'll have to learn how to calm their nerves and get on with the show. That's easy to tell my teenagers, not so easy with six- to nine-year-olds.

"I'm worried, Miss Lyric. What if I forget all the moves?" Kianna asks.

"You won't. You've got this." I look across the room at the rest of the tiny dancers. "You all do. We've practiced all the steps."

"Can we practice again?" Violet, one of my quieter students, inquires. Her ash-blond hair is piled high on her head in an elaborate updo done by her mother, and she's wearing the most adorable pink tutu.

"Of course we can." I pull my phone from my back pocket and quickly swipe for one of my ballet songs. Then I sweep my arms upward and get into first position and the girls follow suit. I walk them through the dance.

It's Kianna who surprisingly moves to the front to lead the dancers in her age group. She effortlessly sways back and forth like a swan, and I can't help but be proud of the progress she's made in only a few months.

I knew she could do it.

Afterward, I take a quick swig of water, when I see Mama and Daddy waving from the door.

"Good luck tonight, babydoll!" Mama gives me a quick kiss and hug.

"Isn't it break a leg?" Daddy asks.

I chuckle. "It doesn't matter. I'm just glad you're both here."

"We didn't come alone," Mama says, and moves aside so I can see Jeremy standing behind them. "We found him wandering around outside and introduced ourselves."

Jeremy shrugs. "You never told me your parents were white."

"Did I have to?" I respond with a smile. "I said they love and support me and that's all the matters. Right?"

He nods in understanding. "Absolutely." Jeremy turns to Mama and Daddy. "You've raised a wonderful daughter. She's graciously invited me to tonight's show."

Mama smiles broadly at his use of the word *daughter*. "That's our Lyric. She has an open heart."

Jeremy looks at me with such heartfelt hope that tears spring to my eyes. "Yes, she does."

"Come and sit with us," my father says.

"I would appreciate that. Thank you kindly." I watch as my parents and my biological father leave the backstage area together.

Learning about my biological family has been so complex and riddled with anxiety. But so far Jeremy and I are off to a good start. He's actually willing to put in a little effort to get to know me, and that means everything.

It's made me realize family isn't about whether we're related or not. Family is who I make it with and who I choose. I'd hoped that my family might someday include Devon and Kianna. I love him and that little girl so much, but if it's not meant to be, I can't force a square peg into a round hole. I will be happy with the family I do have. That's where I belong.

Charity, one of my dance instructors at LT Dance Academy approaches me. "It's time, Lyric."

I clap my hands. "Then let's do the damn thing."

Once the last troupe have their bow, my entire ensemble of dancers return to the stage for their final bow per our rehearsal. That's when Charity makes an announcement.

"We want to give a big thank-you to our fearless leader, the owner and head instructor, everyone please welcome Lyric Taylor to the stage."

Surprised by the gesture, I move forward. The lights hit me, giving me a moment's pause. I used to love the thrill of being on stage. It's not like it used to be, with me as prin-

cipal lead, yet somehow that's okay because I'm helping a
new group of dancers achieve their dreams.

I move forward, and Charity hands me a bouquet of
flowers and a microphone.

"Thank you, thank you," I respond when the crowd is
on their feet giving me a loud standing ovation. I keep the
tears at bay, burning the backs of my eyes.

"Please give another round of applause to our amazing
young dancers." I motion to my students behind me and
give Kianna a wink. "They worked so hard to bring you
this show tonight. And I want to give a special thank-you
to you, the parents, for your tireless efforts in bringing these
dancers to the studio week in and week out. I couldn't do
what I do without your support." I clap my hands. "Give
yourselves a round of applause."

I bow, then take Kianna's and Violet's hands in mine and
move to the front of the stage for one final bow and exit
stage left. Just as I'm doing so, my phone rings, and I see
it's the Gems on a video call.

There's a chorus of "How did it go?"

I smile back at their beautiful faces. "The show went
great. I'm so proud of my students and all their hard work
and dedication."

"And we're proud of you, Lyric," Wynter says, beaming
from ear to ear. "I'm sorry I couldn't be there with you."

"It's fine," I say. "It's just a recital."

"One of many," Teagan responds.

"Hear! Hear!" Shay adds, and holds up a glass of what
looks like champagne. That's when I notice all the girls
have one.

"You guys..." Tears start to slide down my cheeks.

"I think you're missing your own glass," a masculine voice says from behind me. Devon stands there holding a glass of champagne out to me. I accept it and turn to the Gems.

"Congratulations, diva!" Egypt yells.

"Thank you." After a quick toast with the Gems, I end the call to focus on the gorgeous man in front of me.

I'd forgotten how easily Devon can set my heart ablaze with just one look.

"Way to go, Lyric!" Devon leans over and squeezes my shoulders. "I'm so proud of you." When he pulls away, I feel the absence of his heat, the absence of him, and it feels wrong.

Why is he here? To twist the knife and make me see what I can never have? It's cruel, but he is Kianna's father so I put on a brave face.

"Thank you."

"Can we talk?" Devon asks.

"Now?" I ask incredulously, looking around the crowded backstage. "I have dancers to help and parents to thank."

"Later then," he whispers as several dancers come up and hug me. "I'll wait for you."

Then I'm whisked away as parents congratulate me and a few more want to know about enrolling their son or daughter in my next session. The entire night is overwhelming. First my biological father showing up. I mean, yes, I told him about the recital, but I didn't think he would actually come to a kids' performance. Yet he came because of me. Then the recital and seeing all the time and effort I've put in to help my dancers achieve success. The Gems' phone call. And now Devon.

He's here.

Waiting for me.

I'm not sure what to do with that.

I want to rail at him, but I also want to run into his arms and beg him to hold me and never let me go.

Even though I'm loved by my adoptive parents and my friends, I think somewhere deep down I thought I was somehow unlovable because my biological parents didn't want to keep me, but I know now that is far from the case. They were just two high school teenagers who made mistakes and didn't know how to handle them.

Despite it all, I ended up with wonderful, loving parents. I'm blessed. Which is why I can't accept less than what I want, less than I what deserve. I need love, commitment, marriage and all the in between. And if Devon can't give that to me, I'll have to find someone who will.

Devon waits for me in the manager's office of the theater. It was the only place they could give me to have a little privacy before tonight's recital. He spins around to face me and I notice he's holding one of my ballet shoes.

"Are you interested in those for yourself or for Kianna?" I inquire.

He laughs. "Neither." He stands upright. "I was actually thinking about what a big role dance has played in my life. For good and bad."

"But mostly bad," I add.

He shakes his head. "You've brought goodness into my

life, Lyric. Into Kianna's life. I never even knew she wanted
to pursue dance until my sister took her to your studio. I
tried to fight what that meant because my past held too
many unresolved hurts. But seeing Kianna on the stage tonight was thrilling. I've never been so proud, except maybe
when you walked across the stage and took a bow."

I lower my head. "You don't have to flatter me, Devon.
The recital is over. I'll understand if you want to take Kianna out of the studio and find someplace else for her to
study the craft."

"Why would I do that when she's thriving with you?
Because of you."

"You don't mean that."

"Don't I?" he asks, coming closer to me. His familiar,
delicious scent infiltrates my senses and weakens my knees.
"I want to apologize for the way I've handled things. Our
breakup made me see that I was dead inside until I met you
in Aruba. You brought me back to life, Lyric. I was living
in some sort of fog, constantly in pain from the past instead
of dealing with it and moving on, for me and my daughter."

"You were hurting."

"I was hiding," Devon responds. "Hiding from living. I
thought I was broken inside from my failed marriage, but
then you came into my life like a ray of sunshine. You light
up everything and everyone around you. I couldn't help
but fall for you."

My breath hitches in my throat at his words. Surely he
can't mean...

"You made me see what it was like to live again. To have

hope of finding someone special. And I did find someone special. With you, Lyric.

"But—" I blink because I'm not sure I can believe what Devon is saying.

"Please don't give up on us. I love you, Lyric. I think I knew it when we were in Aruba and I was afraid to let you go. I think I knew it when I saw you with your father and incorrectly assumed he was your lover. But I don't think it anymore, I know it. You made me love again, and I'm sorry I was too afraid to see it, sorry I forced us to spend time apart. I was just scared and afraid of letting love in, but I don't want to be afraid anymore."

I place my hand over his mouth, to stop his words. "Don't you think I was scared, too? I'd never felt the kind of passion I had with you with anyone else. It frightened me because of its intensity."

"Me, too. Yet somehow you saw something in me."

I nod. "I did. I saw a man capable and worthy of love."

Devon grasps both my hands and brings them to his lips. "And I want to be worthy of you. You have given me everything I didn't know was possible, but am so grateful I found. I want us to be a family, Lyric. You, me and Kianna. Please say you want that, too."

I weep aloud and nod my head. Devon pulls me into his embrace. He grasps both sides of my face and kisses me through the tears. "I love you, Lyric."

"And I love you, Devon." I tell him the words that have been in my heart for months. Words I want to shout from the rooftops to anyone and everyone who will listen.

"I'm sorry about our time apart. I was a fool, but I vow

I will never leave your side again. I will love you until the world stops turning."

"Kiss me."

And he does, with a fierce passion that leaves me in no doubt of his love for me. I curl my arms around his neck and cling to him. Devon suddenly lifts me from the desk and onto the counter behind me. He kisses me until we're breathless and coming up for air.

That's when we hear a small voice say. "Daddy? Miss Lyric?"

Kianna stands in the doorway with a shocked expression on her face while Chantel grins behind her like a cat that got the cream.

I try to spring away from Devon, embarrassed at having been caught in a lip-lock by a six-year-old, but Devon won't let me go. He merely slides his arm around my waist.

"Are you guys a couple again?" Kianna asks.

"Again?" I'm bewildered at her question.

Kianna nods. "I saw you kiss Daddy a few times when you thought I wasn't looking. And your car was parked outside the house most nights when I went to bed. *All night.*"

A wild blush creeps up my cheeks, and I know I must be as red as an apple.

Devon merely laughs. "Well, you found us out, peanut, because yes, Miss Lyric and I are a couple again. And I'm hoping she might become a part of our family someday. What do you think about that?"

"Really?" Kianna asks excitedly. "I would love it." She rushes over to me and Devon and hugs both of us. "Would you come live with us?"

"If that's what you want," I respond.

"Yay!" Kianna cheers.

I can't be any happier than I am at this moment. The man I love loves me back. And I've finally found the place where I belong.

★ ★ ★ ★ ★

Look for Teagan's story
Break Point
Available February 2025

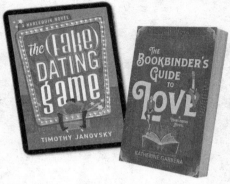